The Flowering Almond Rod

The Story of Trui Straatman,
a courageous believer in
Christian Education

Ge Verhoog

Translated from the original
Dutch by Hendrika Bouw Schuld
and Evelyn Sterenberg

FriesenPress

Suite 300 - 990 Fort St
Victoria, BC, Canada, V8V 3K2
www.friesenpress.com

Copyright © 2015 by Evelyn Sterenberg
First Edition — 2015

Cover Painting by W. TenHam.
Jacoba Geertruida Straatman 1827 - 1905. Portrait by Gaart Beumer.

All rights reserved.

No part of this publication may be reproduced in any form, or by any means, electronic or mechanical, including photocopying, recording, or any information browsing, storage, or retrieval system, without permission in writing from the publisher.

ISBN
978-1-4602-6750-9 (Hardcover)
978-1-4602-6751-6 (Paperback)
978-1-4602-6752-3 (eBook)

1. *Religion*

Distributed to the trade by The Ingram Book Company

Jacoba Geertruida Straatman 1827 - 1905 by Gaart Beumer

Aaron's staff, which represented the house of Levi, had not only sprouted but had budded, blossomed and produced almonds.

–Numbers 17:8 NIV

Jacoba Geertruida Straatman defied the law to begin a school in 1870 in her farmhouse near Harskamp in the Veluwe district of the Netherlands. Her ambition was to enable the children in her neighborhood to read the Bible for themselves. Author Ge Verhoog named the story after the flowering almond rod, because the branch looks dead before it blooms – a spiritual symbol for the life and work of "Trui" Straatman.

This humble widow, unnoticed by most, laid the foundation for a "School with the Bible" in Harskamp. From a small start, the school grew large, and in 1970 was replaced by a prominent modern building in Harskamp on the Veluwe. The author was inspired by the inscription on the cornerstone: "School With the Bible 1901 – New Building 1970." Trui lived her last years with her daughter Jannetje in Ede until her death in 1905. She wrote many letters to Mr. Kamerling and the family Brederveld in Ymuiden.

The Flowering Almond Rod

INTRODUCTION

In one sentence, Geertruida Straatman's purpose in creating a Christian school was that "De kinderen moeten uit de Bijbel kunnen lezen" (The children must be able to read the Bible for themselves). This conviction encapsulates two major themes that characterized the Reformed community in the Netherlands throughout the nineteenth century, namely a devout personal piety, and a biblical-reformed worldview. In the narrative of "Trui" Straatman and her hard-won accomplishment of establishing a "School with the Bible" near Harskamp, the Netherlands, these two Reformed themes play out in an everyday setting to form a piece of the groundwork of the Christian Day School Movement.

The history of the Reformed Church in the Lowlands reveals a consistent theme of the importance the Dutch placed in direct reading of the Bible for the common person. As one of the countries with a relatively high literacy rate in Europe in the sixteenth century, the people of the Netherlands found deep resonance with the message of the Protestant reformers, who advocated for vernacular Bibles and lay reading. Combined with an attraction to the Reformed theology taught by Calvin in Geneva and proclaimed in "hedge" preaching (preaching in open fields), this desire to read the Bible firsthand, and a more personal relationship with God, played a part in the gradual formation of Reformed congregations. Under the leadership of William of Nassau and supported by the Reformed community, the Dutch were quickly engaged in the Eighty Years War (1568-1648). Their resistance to the Catholic, monarchical control of Spain eventually led to independence for a Dutch Republic in 1648 with the signing of the Peace of Munster. Over the next one hundred and fifty years, the *Nederlands Hervormde Kerk* (the Dutch Reformed Church) became firmly established in the Netherlands.

In the nineteenth century, the Reformed Church in the Netherlands would experience two renewal movements: the *Afscheiding* (Separation or Secession) of 1834, and the *Doleantie* (the aggrieved church) of 1888. The Synod of 1816 proved to be a critical event that, in retrospect, catalyzed the first movement to affect the church. This Synod, called by the Dutch monarch William I, instituted a new church order or governance that in effect brought the Reformed Church of the Netherlands under more control of the political state. The new order created governing boards in which all members (mostly clergy) were appointed directly by the king, rather than members who were elected and/or delegated by the people of the church. Thus the clergy, who were already receiving their salary from the state, were even more inclined to practice their office and make decisions that were primarily favourable to the king's wishes.

Another important decision of the Synod was a change in wording of the Form of Subscription (a document pastors signed to pledge their allegiance to the creeds and confessions of the church). The original form required preachers to adhere to the confessional standards *"Because* they accurately reflected the Bible." The revised form stipulated that pastors adhere to confessional standards *"In so far as* they reflected the Bible." The subtle but substantial change opened the door for more individualistic interpretations and preaching of the Bible. These developments initiated at the early nineteenth-century Synod planted the seeds that, in the opinion of many, would lead to church leadership and laity conformed too comfortably close to secular culture. A desire and call for spiritual renewal within the church gradually began to grow.

This call for renewal was also fueled by the conviction of many lay people and some clergy in the Dutch Reformed Church that many preachers had become intellectually liberal, influenced by post-French Revolution modernist, rationalist thinking. As a result, their preaching bore fruit in flocks of nominal Christians who viewed Christianity merely as a moral code with Jesus as primary model. Those who were dissatisfied with this development began to converse. The popular, pious movement that resulted – the *Afscheiding* – began in the village of Ulrum under the leadership of Pastor Hendrick de Cock, and resulted in the formation of the *Christelijke Gereformeerde Kerk* (the Christian Reformed Church) in 1834. This group stressed a return to the orthodox Reformed truths of the Bible: confession of sin and divine grace, a simple trust of Jesus' atoning work and resurrection, and a sincere following in loving obedience. The mentality and spirit of this secession provides a broad background for Trui Straatman's own convictions.

The second pious movement within the Dutch Reformed Church occurred about fifty years later in the form of the *Doleantie*, and provides the immediate historical context in which Trui Straatman fought for a Christian day school. Abraham Kuyper was the primary leader behind the movement. Trained at Leiden University, Kuyper would pastor two congregations, found a Christian University (the Free University in Amsterdam), teach theology, serve in the Dutch Parliament, and eventually become the Prime Minister of the Netherlands (1901-1905). Throughout his career he was a prolific writer, publishing voluminous works on theology, politics, spiritual life, and Christian faith in the form of books, devotionals, and newspaper articles. His influence on the Reformed Church in Holland and beyond is difficult to overestimate. Beginning in the 1870s, Kuyper advocated for renewal in the Dutch Reformed Church in which he served as pastor. The obstacles to his perception of genuine Christian faith he battled included nominal Christianity that he felt was rife in the church; church hierarchical bureaucracy, which he argued stifled the work of the Holy Spirit; and the Enlightenment-inspired liberalism he believed was being preached from many pulpits.

The Flowering Almond Rod

Through his reflections and struggles, Kuyper formulated a Christian faith and understanding that combined a sincere commitment to a personal walk with Jesus with a biblically informed way of understanding society and the world. In 1888 Kuyper led an exodus of about 10% of the Dutch Reformed Church membership in the movement called the *Doleantie*. In 1892 this group joined the church of the *Afscheiding* (the *Christelijke Gereformeerde Kerk*) to form the *Gereformeerde Kerken in de Nederland* (literally the Re-Reformed Church of the Netherlands).

The *Gereformeerde Kerken in Nederland's* emphasis on personal piety and focus on a biblically informed worldview, embodied in Abraham Kuyper and preached from pulpits, found grassroots application in Geertruida Straatman's conviction for building a "School with the Bible": The children must know how to read the Bible for themselves. The ability to read the Bible fostered an immediate, personal relationship with the Lord Jesus, and it revealed a perspective on life and the world opposed to the secular one that Trui found so disturbing and void of meaning. Abraham Kuyper taught that a heart personally devoted to God was absolutely essential to any understanding and application of an intellectual Christian worldview. His meditations, published in daily newspapers, and his *Near unto God* devotional were very popular among the laity. The story of Vrouw Straatman depicts a woman who sought to instill in her pupils the simple and profound trust in God she herself exemplified as she encountered numerous obstacles in building the school. Kuyper's well-known phrase that every square inch of the creation belonged to God, and his frequent use of the term "King Jesus," identifies the second emphasis evident in Trui's commitment to Christian education. Learning was to be done in the context of a biblically informed faith. Life experience was to be viewed through the Christian narrative of creation, fall, and redemption. And the God who created the universe in his sovereign will and power called each child to engage in creation and culture to reflect the presence of his kingdom. Trui taught her students that reading newspapers, history books, and novels was necessary in their responsibility to be fully informed and properly equipped to bear testimony to God's renewing work in the world. She dedicated her adult life to the building of a day school in Harskamp, because she believed it to be a primary instrument through which this hopeful perspective (world and life view) could be ingrained in children as they grew in their faith and trust of their saving Lord Jesus.

The editorial background of *The Flowering Almond Rod* reflects the convictions of three women who believe the story of Christian day schools needs to be retold and remembered. The original Dutch story was published in a Christian weekly newspaper, *The Christian Courier*, in 1970. The author, G.Verhoog, had been impressed by the formidable nature and extraordinary feats of a "simple" woman who was given a vision for the children of her village. These newspaper articles were then translated into

English and compiled into a book by Harriet Schuld (nee Hendrika Bouw), a woman who immigrated to Canada from the Netherlands in 1933. Harriet's resolve that the story should be available to an English-reading, North American audience helped her overcome the challenges of translating a book in her later stages of life into a language that was not her mother tongue. The version you hold in your hand is a transcribed edition written by Harriet Schuld's daughter, Evelyn Sterenberg. Evelyn has rewritten the work of her mother to present a story that is now articulated in fluent vernacular English and easily accessible to any who are interested in a multidimensional account of a small village committed to building a Christian school.

This work may be characterized as a historical novel. It is a reconstruction of actual events based on sources the author and subsequent researchers used, such as records of school business and building plans and discussions found in archives, oral accounts, and personal letters written by Straatman. Through these sources, the author has presented the character and convictions of the protagonist: a picture of a woman with pioneering vision, indefatigable perseverance, and a sunny disposition grounded in a sincere faith. However, the narrative engagingly recreates numerous other Harskamp personalities and their efforts to establish and grow a school, along with a few other colourful figures outside of the village who also played key parts. Anyone today interested and involved in the formal education of children, in a snapshot of one instance in the history of

Christian education, in everyday life in nineteenth-century small village Netherlands, or in the relationship of Christian faith and society and raising children in our world, would find this popular history a worthy read. *The Flowering Almond Rod* is an enlightening historical example of devout faith and a Christian worldview as it was expressed and embodied in everyday characters, small-town community dynamics, entertaining anecdotes, and ultimately in the glowing faces of children who first learned to read in a farmhouse school near the Dutch town of Harskamp.

Tony Maan

CHAPTER ONE

The Inspector Visits the Veluw

With muffled step, the horse's feet move over the dry sandy trails of the Veluwe. The hot summer sun beats down. The blooming heather and the low shrubs lie still in the midday heat. The old nag plods on, her head hanging low, over the twisting trail through the soft white sand. The sky is clear blue. The man on the horse periodically takes out his big white handkerchief to wipe his brow. In the distance, dark fringes of spruce promise relief from the sun.

"What a trek!" de heer van Limmen muses, "If I were a sultan, I would have a pajong (coolie) with a fan to cool me, but I am only a school inspector. It is an honorable position, but I feel more like an explorer."

He thinks about all the inventions of the past few years. First there was the railroad train and now there is talk about a velocipede. People in Holland call it a "fiets." Where will it all end? People think they know it all. Blind Peter said it must be the devil – two wheels turning behind each other with a man between. Eight years ago today in 1869, there was a bicycle race in France. The papers wrote about it – a distance of 126 kilometers, won by an Englishman at twelve kilometers per hour! Such speed, it takes your breath away! No, a horse is much safer. A horse knows exactly what speed a person needs and obeys the reins.

A few hours pass and at last some small low buildings appear. Poor little farms, so different from the wide grain fields of Limburg, Friesland, and South Holland. But these people of Gelderland seem to be satisfied. Limmen notes the low-hanging thatched roofs and the walls with their small windows. Inside each building there would be a middle door separating the living quarters from the barn. The sheepcote huddles beside the barn. Light wisps of smoke hang in the air in the trees beyond the buildings.

Limmen turns his mind to the purpose of his trip. It has been rumored that these isolated people have a secret school system. The area is so sparsely populated it is not worth providing a school for the few pupils who would also have to help with seeding, weeding, and haying much of the year. Occasionally a retired sailor or peddler provides a book and a rod for the children. Less often, a genuine government-authorized teacher might appear. The wages are low, so a teacher must also serve as gardener, bell-ringer, and greaser of the church clock. Also as song leader and funeral director. Each funeral earns the teacher a bushel of rye. And then there is the yearly egg collection. At Easter he could go from farm to farm with a basket to be filled with eggs – a free meal for his family. A teacher was well off and could also enjoy other people's children all his life. And yet you still meet complainers – incredible! In Amsterdam, for example, there is a school where the teacher must work under a third-story roof, scorching hot in the summer and icicles on the rafters in winter. Two hundred children, steep stairs, and a trap door to keep watch that they are working at their studies. A teacher should be satisfied to work on the Veluwe.

Yet Limmen must see that education is carried out according to regulations. Where there is a school, he has to investigate, and a trip like this may lead to discoveries. It seems there is something not quite right here. He travels slowly toward Ede on the gravelly path. A few children stand at the side of the road.

"Can you tell me the name of the next village?" he asks.

The boys stand, their hands in the pockets of their baggy black pants. They wear blue-and-white-striped shirts and white klompen. Unruly yellow hair peeks out from little flat caps. The girls wear striped pinafores over dark dresses, their legs in black hand-knitted stockings, feet in klompen. Straggly hair hangs from little straw hats. Boys and girls alike are shy of the stranger.

One is brave enough to ask, "Where are you going?"

"I did not ask you that. I want you to tell me if I'm coming to Ede soon!"

The children nod and point in one direction – of course, Ede is that way.

"And what is the name of this place?"

What a nosy man! "That's our little house, and the other is the place of old Gees and—" They stop short. "Do you want to call on old Trui, perhaps?"

What a forsaken place, and old Trui? Never heard of her. Limmen wonders, "Who is she?"

The children inform him eagerly, "That's old Trui from the school, and we go to school at her place there, sir." All hands point to a small frame house with a thatched roof, wide board walls, and white plastered front living quarters. The cows and sheep live in the back in the usual way. Tall thinly leaved trees shelter one side. Poverty is evident.

"What did you tell me? Is there a school here? Where is it?"

"There in that house, that's old Trui's school."

Astonished, Limmen turns to the house. What will he discover here in the hinterland? "And what is the name of this place?"

"Harskamp," replies a child importantly, "And old Trui's name is Trui of Harskamp!"

"Is that her family name?"

All shoulders and noses rise as if to say, who knows? Go and ask her.

Limmen turns to the house. He wants to meet her. Harskamp... no, it is not on the official school list. Perhaps it is one of those dreadful unauthorized classes. The nearest public school is in Otterloo. The sunny quietness of a midsummer afternoon hangs over the farmhouse as he dismounts and surveys the smallholding with its single small-paned window. A black-tarred strip separates the white front of the house from the white sand below. A little barn leans against the house seemingly for support. The muffled cackling of chickens sounds from the barn. An old wood-handled pump stands near the door, a pail on its hook. Around it, stones keep the ground from getting muddy.

Limmen raps with his cane, the top half of the Dutch door opens, and a woman faces him. She looks like the usual Veluwe farm wife – a round face with fine features, small mouth, and clear open eyes. A ruffled bonnet covers most of her head, but a few grey hairs parted in the center and pasted flat can be seen. The bonnet, with its pleated back ruffle, is homemade, carefully washed, and starched, is typical of those worn by the women of the region. Her shapeless figure is brisk, her dress is black with a white collar, and a blue and white cotton apron covers her full hips. Placing her hands on the bottom half of the door, she peers at the stranger. "Well?" she inquires.

Limmen holds his cane like a weapon, his other hand in his pocket. He is impressed. "My destination is Ede," he begins, then feels his confidence wane as he faces this courageous woman. He chides himself for being impressed by a woman. He moves closer, balancing his cane. "Yes, vrouwtje, little lady, I got lost and I don't know the name of this dorpje."

"Dorpje? Don't you know this is Harskamp? It is a good place to live. I was born here and never travelled further. Why should I? I can walk to Apeldoorn across the heather to listen to a good minister, but my home is here."

"A satisfying existence, I suppose."

"Why not? I have a cow and a goat and a piece of land. But was there something you wanted to know?"

"Oh, nothing special. The children tell me that you teach them. That's hard to believe. Maybe I am wrong."

She smiles, "That's true. I am Trui of Harskamp."

"Your husband's name is...?"

"My name is Jacoba Geertruida Straatman. My husband's name is Jan Heebink."

"Your husband keeps the school?"

"My man died, let me see, ten years ago! In '67. He caught cold. He was only forty-four years old, and I was left with five children. If the Lord had not been with me...."

"Did you remarry?"

"Oh no, why should I? I am busy enough, but I understand. Besides my farm work, I teach the children. Do you want to see the school?" With short steps, she leads him to the back of the house, where there is a small space beside the stall. "Look, here is where I keep school."

Astonished, Limmen exclaims, "School?"

She plants her hands on her hips and looks over the place with low benches where thirty children can squeeze in. "Yes, I have to do this. There is no school in Harskamp, and Kootwijk is too far for the children to walk."

"But Otterloo has a public school."

The Flowering Almond Rod

Trui nods. "That's true, but I think children who are baptized should go to a Christian school." She looks at him expectantly.

"Yes, but the public school is not against religion."

"You think so? Well, I don't." Stubbornly, she presses her lips together. "I speak from experience. I was converted from an ungodly life when I was thirty-four, and then I understood that there is only happiness when I personally know the Bible and what it contains. That's why children should learn to read. That's why I teach children reading — so they can understand the Bible."

"How do you teach reading?"

Trui points to a little book with a red rooster on its cover. "From the rooster book. It's a good book because it has all the letters with their pronunciation. It works fine."

"The rooster book...." Limmen knows it. It was in use in the early 1700's, printed more than a hundred years ago and used widely. He remembers the title page:

> Men moet in het A.B.C. geoefend wezen,
>
> Eer men in eenige Boeken iets kan lezen
>
> This ABC book you need
>
> If you want to learn to read.

But he wonders how a simple farm woman in a corner of a barn can teach anything. "So you did this for several years?"

"More than seven years, and I will keep on teaching until we have a Christian school here."

He scoffs. "You are dreaming. This town is too small, and schools cost money."

Trui is irritated. "You are right, sir, to think that it is costly to be a Christian. Yet I cannot understand why in a Christian nation there is no government support for Christian schools, but only for education without religion." She plants her hands on her hips. "I am convinced a time will come when our government supports Christian education."

He smiles, amused. "I don't share your opinion, vrouwtje. Public education has strong support, and it is sufficient for all citizens. Why spend a fortune on any other kind of school?"

Trui pities him. "Some feel there is no need for Christianity. That's why we have to manage for ourselves. I have read that faith is an offence to a Greek and foolishness to a Jew. Believers may seem to be fools, but one thing is certain – God is the strength of life, and poor are those who struggle on without Him. That is why I keep teaching the children and also teach their parents in the evenings."

Limmen ponders; people who have religion are often unreasonable. It irritates him. He cannot understand why people let themselves be oppressed by an age-old Jewish book. He shakes his head. "What else do you teach the children?"

"Arithmetic is something I don't understand, so that is out. I teach reading and writing, memory work, and history."

"But the children need arithmetic too!" As inspector of schools, he is annoyed that children have such a limited education and that the law allows this. It's a good thing he got lost and found out what goes on.

"I teach what is necessary. They learn to figure by themselves."

Slowly Limmen returns to his waiting horse.

"Possibly you could do something to build a school here...."

"I'll think about it," Limmen replies as he mounts and rides toward the village.

Trui shakes her head. Not much to hope for from that fellow. He does not know God. How can he understand her need? She looks at the clear blue sky. There's where my help will come from. God helps His children and shelters them like the hills around Jerusalem shelter the city.

Limmen spurs his horse to greater speed. He wants to reach Ede for a meeting tonight. He still wonders about the strange situation in Harskamp. The poor children have only an uneducated woman who thinks she can teach. That evening he talks with fellow board members, glad to meet with his equals. There is a spare room ready for him, so they have time to talk business. They smoke long-stemmed pipes, the lady of the house makes tea, and all have a pleasant evening.

The Horstmans entertain with such charm. They are influential people, prominent in business. "We live in interesting times," begins Horstman. "This is the century of development. Last century was the end of the Golden Age. Holland's superior position was shaken by the French Revolution."

Limmen refills his pipe. "You are so right. The authorities in this country are righting many injustices with great ambition."

Horstman agrees. "It is wonderful to be active in creating justice."

Mevrouw Horstman adds, "I am so glad you are busy caring for your neighbors' well-being. Not many are willing to spend time or money for it anymore."

"It is my duty," replies Horstman. "This is how we maintain national unity. When the rich are generous and the poor are thankful, knowing their place and living quietly, we can maintain a just society. We must not change the natural order."

"I happened to wander over the Veluwe," Limmen begins. "In the afternoon, I came to the village of Harskamp. I didn't know the Veluwe was so huge. What an endless stretch! It was interesting to see the variety of brush, heather, and sandy trails. The landscape went on and on endlessly. The sun was merciless, but the cool evening eased my discomfort. Here and there I saw poor farmsteads with just a few acres of sandy soil. I wondered if the people were very poor out there, but I suppose poverty is not the right term. They expect little and are satisfied. They aren't aware of anything better, I suppose. They don't know about the rich clay soil in the polders, reclaimed from the sea. Just think of the Haarlemmermeer. That's been dry for twenty-five years now. But the pace of life never changes on the Veluwe."

"Yes, it is quite isolated," agrees Horstman. "They don't know what happens in the rest of the country. Anyhow, they seem more interested in religion than in newspapers and city life." He laughs. "They make a living on their dry ground with a flock of sheep, a couple of goats, and some chickens. They exist on that, and it keeps the country's economy balanced."

Limmen graciously accepts another cup of tea. "I met an old woman in Harskamp. I forget her name...."

"That must be Trui of Harskamp – Old Trui, Trui Straatman."

Limmen tells of his encounter. "She teaches children, and being the school inspector, I was interested."

"Oh, yes," Horstman agrees. "The last of her kind. That sort of people disappears and their works don't follow them. Let them be. Trui is old and will soon be forgotten."

"She certainly does not seem to be dying yet," Limmen interrupts. "She is so old fashioned, I am glad we don't see much of her kind of teaching any more. Our government promotes education, and I am reminded of Van Swinderen, who wanted to get rid of uneducated emergency teachers."

Horstman straightens in his chair. "You remember the time when farm children had to stay home in the summer to work in the field? Trui keeps the country school going for a few in the summer. It's amusing to know how those country schools fared. Fifty to seventy children in one room, with very little discipline."

"The teacher did everything by himself," Limmen adds, "But only for the money."

" Yes, they were more materialistic than idealistic. Were the salaries adequate?"

"Well," he makes himself comfortable in the armchair, "I remember a call for a teacher in Nunen. It was around 1820, salary two hundred guilders a year. He also received pay for acting as bell ringer and funeral director at thirty-six cents per funeral."

"It's a good thing the government has taken responsibility now for education. We need consistency in this country."

"You are quite right, but will it work? Hollanders are so independent."

"We have laws and we can always make more laws for the benefit of the children, the next generation."

Limmen notices through the high windows that the evening is looming. The leaves of the tall trees do not stir, and the flowers spread their fragrance. "Old Trui mentioned the benefit to the children, too," he observes slowly. "She feels the children do not receive what they need in the public school."

"Oh, so what?" Impatiently, Horstman rubs the carved armrest of his comfortable chair. "The people of the Veluwe are religious fanatics. Instead of keeping up with modern thought, they hold tightly to the values of ancient times. They are so narrow-minded!"

"I noticed that on my journey this afternoon. People are like that when they live in isolation, totally ignorant of new development. They never go beyond their homes and yards and poor sandy fields. Don't expect broadmindedness. Their opinion is the only one; they hold the Bible in their hands and minds. That old book is all they know, and they don't care about anything else."

"But those people can make a lot of trouble," prophesies Horstman. "Trui seems meek, but she will fight for her ideals." With the stem of his pipe, he points at his guest. "And with her there are many parents dissatisfied with our education. Think about the Christian School Society. They want to take over the public schools, add their Biblical perspective, and declare that to be the right system. They are supported by Groen van Prinsterer, a member of the government's second chamber." His face reddens with irritation and excitement over the notion that the Christians of the nation have become so rebellious.

Mevrouw Horstman senses the tension in the air. Her husband is usually calm and contained, but he occasionally loses his temper. She tries to calm things down with offers of coffee and wine. She smiles as the offer is accepted.

Limmen is pleased when the maid brings in the bottle and glasses. He is appreciative of women who stay in their place and don't interfere with men's business. Especially not in social problems such as the difficulty of dealing with persons like Trui of Harskamp. It is not appropriate for a lady of position.

He expresses his thoughts. "A good woman is the crown of the home," he observes, intending to compliment his hostess. "Let us hope to be spared the evil of emancipation. Just imagine, women who think they belong in spheres created strictly for men. Just think – what was her name again? That fanatic woman who should be locked up – Alletta Jacobs, a woman doctor! She is seeking certification!" He lifts his glass toward the oil lamp and enjoys the sparkling glow. "I cannot see those women succeeding. Men will have to uproot those weeds in our Netherlands gardens." He swallows a goodly sip of wine. We'll keep a sharp eye on the situation, he tells himself.

Before he expresses this thought aloud, mevrouw Horstman observes, "Still, this vrouw Straatman – old Trui as she is called – is to be admired for her work. She works well with the children and she likes helping them. Maybe women such as she understand children and therefore make good teachers." She stops, amazed to hear herself speaking so boldly.

Limmen listens graciously. This woman is not one to have foolish ideas in her head. She is a respectable wife and mother. Such statements coming from her are inappropriate but also amusing.

"Those amateur psychologists," he chuckles. "I agree, they may develop insight into character through daily contact with children, insight a graduate might envy.

They must, however, be kept under control by the inspectors. With my experience, I can correct and prevent many mistakes. We will have to watch Trui carefully. She has to realize she may be allowed to take in children, play games with them, and have them help her with the sheep and goats. But, after all, she is a just a poor lonely widow, and she should not think herself capable of teaching." He shakes his head. "She is going too far for me to ignore. She admits herself that the children don't learn arithmetic."

The discussion continues complacently as the content of the wine bottle disappears. The hours fly by. The pendulum under the glass dome and the gilded shepherd pointer indicate a late hour. It is time for bed. They realize there is much work to be done, so much illiteracy in the land yet. What can be done about it? Maybe there ought to be a law to enforce education for all children. But a lot of water will flow into the sea before that happens.

Ge Verhoog

CHAPTER TWO

Trui's Conversion

Trui has finished her evening rounds. The cow is lying down, the goat is content, the chickens are on their roost, and the shutters are closed over the windows. She makes this round every evening and morning. The moon-shaped cutouts in the shutters enable her to see the dawn arrive. She slips out of her bed-closet into the room. Time is precious; the days are short. A few strokes of the pump handle bring fresh rushing water into the stone trough. She washes her hands and cheeks until they glow. Then she places her white starched muslin bonnet over her greying hair and ties the bow neatly under her chin. She nods at her reflection in the cracked spotty mirror.

"Well, Trui, another day to be useful," she says to herself. Every day has enough joy and trouble. In winter, school means extra work, but now in midsummer the children are home, with the sheep on the heather, or out planting seedling pines. Summer is the time for gardening in her little plot and for selling eggs and milk for a few pennies.

Trui has been a widow for many years. Her oldest daughter Mina is married to Gerrit van Ee. Gerritje is next in the family, and then Kornelis. He is twenty and is courting Evertje from Ede. Next is Gerrit, secretive about what he does with his free time, but this may not be a bad thing. Jannetje, the youngest, is fourteen and works away from home, which means she brings in some money, too. Trui worries about her children.

She plants her hands on her hips and looks over the small yard. She came here as the joyful bride of Jan Heebink, and they had sixteen happy years together. The children came one after the other. She remembers their shrieks of laughter as they played among the chickens. She sees her sturdy, faithful husband Jan, whom she had to lay in the graveyard. She shakes her head and goes inside.

The boys are still asleep in the attic. Jannetje's little room is above the low storage cellar. Trui's bed is in a closet-like alcove, so common in the homes of Holland. On a shelf above the bed is her much-used Gedichten (Poems) by Ds. Sluyter. She reads a poem every night, along with a Bible chapter. She loves the poetry for itself, not just because her husband brought it home one day after finding it in an old attic. He appreciated his wife's curious mind.

"Look what I found! It is old and crumbly, but I think you will like it," he said. "Gedichten" by Willem Sluyter, born 1620." What a long time ago!

"Minister in Eibergen," Trui reads. Eibergen – that's in east Gelderland. How does a book like that end up here?

The Flowering Almond Rod

It must be good. The language is plain and clear, the writing is precise, and the poems are about ordinary things.

> "If you want peace and rest, where do you look?
> In a corner with a book.
> Look here or there and where thou wilt,
> Thou will find it in the stilte (silence)."

She feels so happy to have this little book, remembering how Jan smiled on his way to work, confident of his gift. He was not sure he could understand why the Bible suddenly meant so much to her, but it did no harm. She looked after the children, he had his food and drink; she was a good wife.

Trui keeps the precious book beside the big Bible with its brass clasps, which she reads every day. She must catch up on so many lost years. She found the Lord at the age of thirty-four. Then she knew what God wanted from her and she saw what mattered most. She always felt there must be a purpose for being born. She will never forget the day of her conversion. She was never very religious, even though the people of the Veluwe were known for their heavy-hearted faith. Isolation, loneliness, and hard work on lean soil kept them poor, looked down upon by business and industrial entrepreneurs. Depression dulled their minds.

Trui, however, was never depressed. She wanted to know the purpose of life. As a young girl, she would not accept the idea that fate ruled and life ended in the grave.

Jan Heebink was amused – purpose of life? You have the children, so don't mope.

Yes, the children, what about them? How can I protect them? What will become of them?

Jan's response was to assure her that with her for a mother, their future was definitely not the alleys or the gallows.

Life had not been easy for Trui. Before each new baby was to be born, the old women warned, "Every time you go into labor, one foot drags into the grave. Don't you realize that?" The midwife had no answer for Trui's questions. A heavy-hearted elder of the church thought he knew. His words were lead and stone, as weighty as the enormous meals he devoured. He knew the answers because he was saved. He shook his head when Trui peppered him with questions.

"What? A woman must quietly and meekly manage her household. Woman, your pride shows through the rips in your clothes."

Deeply grieved, she went home. "That fool. Pride? Me? That's outright slander."

Jan Heebink just laughed. "Trui, I like this farm. Otherwise I'd suggest we move elsewhere. You don't belong here. Maybe we should pull up stakes. I'm afraid if you keep having run-ins like these, I'll die laughing, and you don't want that, do you?" Suffering and complaints, laughter and happiness, poverty and wealth, sorrow and peace: life had many parts.

The Flowering Almond Rod

The sermons preached in the churches of this impoverished region were also impoverished, too poor for Trui's soul. She could not understand all the lamenting while outside the sun shone. Why moan in church when fat sides of bacon hung in the rafters of homes? Did the people actually enjoy groaning over all the malodorous sins that clung to them? They just kept repeating these sins again and again. However, on a certain Sunday in April 1861, things changed. She will never forget that date.

That Sunday, young Ds. Ploos van Amstel started his career in the church of Otterloo. He was reputed to have special gifts. He had planned to be a bookseller, then a notary, but he became so excited about the Gospel that he had only one wish: to dedicate his life to telling others the good news. Trui walked to Otterloo to hear his very first sermon. His clear eyes and gentle manner impressed her. His cheerful Christian demeanor came from within his soul. She didn't remember much of the sermon, for she did not know the Bible well enough to understand all of it. One thing she did know: this man did not stand there to receive honor for himself. He did not look down on the people as hopelessly lost sinners, but rather gave them hope. He said, "Here we are, Lord. What do you want us to do? Please help us."

He tells us the truth, Trui thought. It is so clear; he answers my questions. I wish I could hear him again. The service ended with a prayer of thankfulness by the newly ordained minister. He expressed his feelings in just a few sentences, but they were sentences filled with depth and emotion. This occasion was the fulfillment of his ambition; finally he had arrived to start his life of service to God. He could now minister to a congregation and put his whole heart into it. "Lord God, I ask but one thing," he prayed, "That I could be a blessing to even one soul. I would know then that my life has been worthwhile."

Please let me be the one, thought Trui. I have searched so long, and what I heard today is so real, so really true.

She arrived at home happy. "Jan, now I know what the Bible means. I am going to read it every day and try to understand it better, and if I don't understand it, I'll ask that minister to help me."

Jan could not understand Trui's excitement, but her behavior and shining eyes told him she had changed. A calm happiness enveloped her, for she had discovered a treasure she would never lose. "I want everyone to be as happy as I am. I cannot keep it to myself and will do anything to explain how rich I became when I first believed in God."

It did not affect Jan, for he had his acres to tend and his beans to water. The pig had to be butchered so there would be smoked pork sides and sausages to hang on the beams for the coming winter. Besides that, there were the sheep and goats. Husband and wife did farm work together, but Trui would have to deal with the religious matters alone. Trui was burdened to know her husband did not share her joy, and also that her children lived a shallow life.

Children... there were so many here in Harskamp who knew very little about the Bible. They were baptized, but how could their parents keep the promise they had made at their baptism to instruct them in the Christian faith? Harskamp had neither church nor minister nor Christian school, and Otterloo was a three-quarters of an hour walk away.

Trui did not mind walking four hours over the heather to Apeldoorn to hear Ds. Braal, a fiery orator who was not only a gifted speaker, but also had excellent ideas. A walk to hear such a speaker was pleasure for her. But she was different from her neighbors on the Veluwe. Her opinions and actions drew attention. Those people felt that women should be dependent on men. Adam was created first, then Eve, and therefore the wife should always walk a few steps behind her husband and not try to emulate men's ideas.

"Foolish girl," said Jan. "Be glad I'm not a strict believer in faith and church, for you would not enjoy the freedom you have now. Our life is good, we have five fine children, and I don't mind you speaking your mind about those rich people." He was a good fellow, her Jan. He understood her.

The clock struck twelve, waking her up from her musing. How did she get lost in her memories? Then she recollects the afternoon when the stranger came to talk to her. Did she tell him too much? Maybe she shouldn't have told him about her school or showed it to him. Why would it be wrong? She sincerely believes that children should be taught about Christianity in school. Still, she feels uneasy about the man's visit. He was too observant, too silent. She can't say why it worries her that he saw it and promised that she'd hear more about it. She knows she is doing the right thing, but if the high and mighty authorities prohibit her from teaching, they should build a school in Harskamp and then she could quit. She smiles inwardly at the thought of the high and mighty. One ought to respect authority, but why do those arrogant people so often make it difficult to respect their power? Why do the cities and towns have government-supported schools, but no schools with the Bible? Why are we laughed at? Are we so foolish? Why must we support schools considered to be normal but are without the Bible, and yet have our desire for Christian schools considered outrageous? Why is the Christian faith hated so much when it has given her a well of happiness?

The religion of the Veluwe does not attract many. Trui knows that from experience. She wanted to be a Christian, but not like the people among whom she lived. The young pastor in Otterloo opened her eyes to a different Christianity. His beaming happiness in Jesus, his courage in everyday life, his confidence that God held everything in His hand spoke to her in a new way. She knew from then on the way she would live.

She thinks about her life. She loved Jan Heebink, but he is gone. He would no longer work their few acres, he would not herd his sheep into the pen, the goat would not bleat when he stepped outside. Jan Heebink, the quiet,

The Flowering Almond Rod

cheerful boy who had courted her. He had understood her. He was only forty-four and she thirty-nine when she was left with five children, the youngest only three and the eldest fifteen. "If I had not believed in God," Trui muses, "If I had not believed, what then?" Still, she wonders if Jan actually did arrive at Heaven's gate. But she has prayed fervently for his salvation, and God has promised to hear the prayers of a believer.

In November 1883 when her last child was born, she was so sick no one expected her to recover. Jan did admit that when her health and strength returned, it was more that a doctor's efforts that healed her. "When you people die, you blame the doctor, and if you recover, it is the by the grace of God," grumbled the doctor. He had a point, but Trui thought differently. In the first place, God had granted the doctor his gift of helping people. That's the reason we call for his help, but ultimately it is God who holds the power of life and death. When butchering time came around, a tasty side of pork for the doctor's table helped to ease his annoyance.

Trui had an idea. There was a way to teach the children of Harskamp about the Bible. Two years after Jan's passing, she organized a space on the red stone floor in her barn. In that space she placed some long backless benches made for her by a local carpenter. "I know for a fact," said the carpenter, "All school benches should be made without back rests. Otherwise the children become soft and lazy. I have a friend in the city who knows somebody from a real school. He told me so, and now I'm telling you."

Trui listened patiently. "And who told you that this won't be a real school?"

"Well, vrouw, that's not what I said."

"I'm sure you will be sending your children."

Silence. "Do I have to?" after a long pause.

Trui nodded her head. "Of course you have to. I was in church when your children were baptized and you and your wife promised to bring them up in the nurture of the gospel. What became of that?"

The carpenter shoved his worn black cap back in sudden anger. "You mean to say I don't bring up my children in a Christian way?"

"They are going to the public school in Otterloo, aren't they?"

"I have no choice. Kootwijk is a hour and a quarter to walk every day through that drifting sand."

Trui nodded. "I see. Some parents don't want their children to walk so far, so they don't go to school at all and will never learn to read. Now remember – there will be classes here all winter on Tuesdays, Thursdays, and Fridays from one to three."

"How are you going to do that?"

"You'll see. I will teach the girls to knit, and both boys and girls will learn reading, writing, songs, and hymns so they can read the Bible and sing."

The carpenter moved his cap back to its normal position. "My, my."

Trui laughed at the stunned look on his face. "Did I scare you?"

"Scare me? No, why should it? If you need me, let me know. However," and he looked directly at her, "I feel you will succeed."

The carpenter related his experience at home, and the news spread quickly. On Saturday night of that same week, Trui donned a clean starched bonnet, her black dress, and her striped apron and walked to the village square, where the men gathered under the spreading oak to discuss the news of church and state. She approached them, relating her plans to start a school at her home. The men listened, for she was well respected for her hard work. People liked her because she never wore others down with complaints, but rather had a witty and cheerful remark for everyone. So the pupils came, and Trui taught them for seven years.

But now this stranger has come to see her school, making her feel uneasy. "Oh, come now," she tells herself. "You're getting old and whiny. You see clouds rising from the Zuider Zee, but that's far from Harskamp. If he makes trouble, just be honest, that's all." She leafs through her Bible, steel-rimmed glasses perched on her nose. She reads till late in the night from the story of Elisha in II Kings 6. "Fear not, those with us are stronger and greater in number than those against us."

Ge Verhoog

CHAPTER THREE

The School Begins

Winter comes early. The children at home are underfoot, doing nothing useful and getting into mischief. It is time for Trui's school to begin. She stands outside, watching them arrive. A pile of lumber donated from someone's dismantled chicken coop lies in the yard. She will have the children bring it into the barn before school starts. Her own son and daughter, Gerrit and Jannetje, must leave for their jobs away from the farm.

"Children, pile the wood neatly in the barn; every scrap is useful. Be very careful." She bustles back and forth giving directions. When the yard is cleared of wood, the children come inside.

Trui counts. Thirty all together, a good start. They quickly find places on the benches. Kaatje screams when her bench wobbles on the uneven floor, but Hannes pushes it level and firm. Most of the children are new. Trui asks their names. From the surnames, Trui can place them in their families. Gijs's father has a fine sheep shed, Jasper's family lives in a sod hut, and Govert's family raises chickens.

Annechien, the oldest of ten, cares and worries written on her face, is from a family weighed down spiritually by their religion. Krelis, her father, burdens himself and his whole family, worrying if they will ever see the light and be converted unto salvation. Then there is Koba, whose parents are sad because they have only the one child. "We're guilty of many sins, that's why the Lord did not trust us with more children."

"Be thankful that the Lord only gave you one to take care of," Trui remarked once. "A big family can be mighty poor." That remark almost cost Koba the opportunity to go to Trui's school. Her father Ariaan struggled fiercely with the decision.

"I have wrestled on my knees with tears, lamenting over the question of whether I should entrust my Koba, my only treasure, to such an arrogant woman as this Trui seems to be." The dilemma was finally resolved when his wife suggested that a daughter who could not read or write would never find a good husband. The school in Harderwijk was too far away, so they had to trust her to Trui.

Trui is amused by Ariaan's lack of consistency. He tramples on his own ideals. Little Koba, with her bristly pigtails, sits between the other girls. Trui longs to bring some happiness to this child and shelter her from the notion that this earth is nothing but a vale of tears.

Woutje, daughter of Klaas, on the other hand, is a cheerful, fine-faced chatterbox. An exceptional child, a sunbeam, she is a lone light flickering in the dark woods.

The Flowering Almond Rod

Klaas migrated from the lowlands, a place much different from the Veluwe. He was used to the boisterous sea wind of the coast. A clever man, but not considered to be one of the elect in this community. He doesn't understand that this world is a place of mourning where death can suddenly appear at the window, and then his bed will be too short and the covers too narrow. He cannot say, "My Father, my Father, I have never known..." for it will be too late. No, Klaas is too happy, he does not have faith, and he is to be pitied by those who think they know the truth. Trui welcomes the opportunity to teach this child to read the Bible.

"Everyone, quiet down," Trui calls the children to order. "We have talked enough, the yard is clean, and now our lessons will begin." She keeps a stick behind the door, but never uses it; its presence is adequate motivation for orderly student behavior. The young faces before her shine with expectation, for the first lesson of the first day of school is an important event in their lives. They have heard so much from older brothers and sisters. Trui does not make the work easy, but they like her just the same. No trace of fear mars their expectation.

"What day is it today?"

"Tuesday," respond many voices.

Trui nods. "Remember, every Tuesday the girls will stay after school for knitting. Next week each of you is to bring four needles and black wool, and we will learn to knit stockings.

"My father knows how to knit," announces Gijs. "He always knits when he herds the sheep."

The rest of the boys are not interested. "We have other things to do – gathering eggs, feeding livestock, hauling manure...."

"And going to school," Trui adds. "Quiet, please." She claps her hands. "The boys do not have to knit. First, we will learn a song." She pulls out a six-cornered harmonium, a wondrous instrument the likes of which they have never seen before. With firm fingers she presses the knobs, then pulls it open and closed rhythmically. A shrill screech erupts from the instrument, followed by a tuneful melody. The children stare, fascinated.

"I'll say the first line of psalm eighty-one, we will all repeat it, and then we will sing it," she announces. "Listen well. 'Open wide your mouth, ask from me believing.'" Together they repeat the lines and then sing them. In spite of the squeaky tones of the old harmonium, Trui's singing voice is unfalteringly true in pitch.

"A psalm is either praise or prayer," she instructs. "What would the Lord think of us if we prayed or praised him with shrill howls?" The children learn quickly, and soon they can sing all the lines from memory. Trui is pleased. "We'll sing this song every school day this week. Next week, a new one, and so you will learn to sing the psalms."

After putting away the instrument, she holds up two booklets. "See these? You will learn to read from these little books. And why should we learn to read?"

The Flowering Almond Rod

No response, some questioning looks.

"Why should you learn to read?" she repeats.

One hand rises tentatively. "You would know, when you buy a cow, if you are being cheated."

Trui removes her spectacles. "You can know that without being able to read. You need a different kind of knowledge for that, which you can learn in the field and barn. Think again – why is reading necessary?"

"When my aunt writes a letter," Woutje suggests, showing off that she has faraway relatives. (Who else would have aunts who write letters?)

"Yes, you are close, my girl," Trui approves. "If your aunt or uncle or grandparent wrote a letter, it would be a shame if you couldn't read it. Now God in Heaven has written letters too. He sent them to us, and they are bound together in the Bible. We cannot do without those letters, because they tell us how to live happy lives and how we can live with God in Heaven after this life. Without reading and writing we would not know these things."

"Why writing?" Woutje asks. "Do we write a letter back to God?"

The other children shudder. That Woutje....

"You can ask any questions," Trui responds as she senses the shudder. "The Lord is pleased when we think about Him, but you don't have to write Him a letter. I am teaching you writing so you can copy and memorize for later use."

She holds up one of the books. "This book is about our nation's history. Those who can already read may look at the questions, and then we'll talk about it." A few children huddle together to read. Some have been taught a little at home, but in general they have pitifully few skills.

For the beginners, she uses the Rooster book. A classic for beginning readers, it features the alphabet in several sizes with sensible examples. She is glad it has none of the "brave Hendrik" moralism. Children are not that good. To portray brats as holy innocents is useless. Reading goes together with moral and personal growth in her school. The Rooster book contains the Lord's Prayer, the Confession, and the Ten Commandments. It also has five prayers to be used morning, evening, at school, before a meal, and after a meal.

The Flowering Almond Rod

Scanned from original documents in
possession of Trui Straatman's descendants.

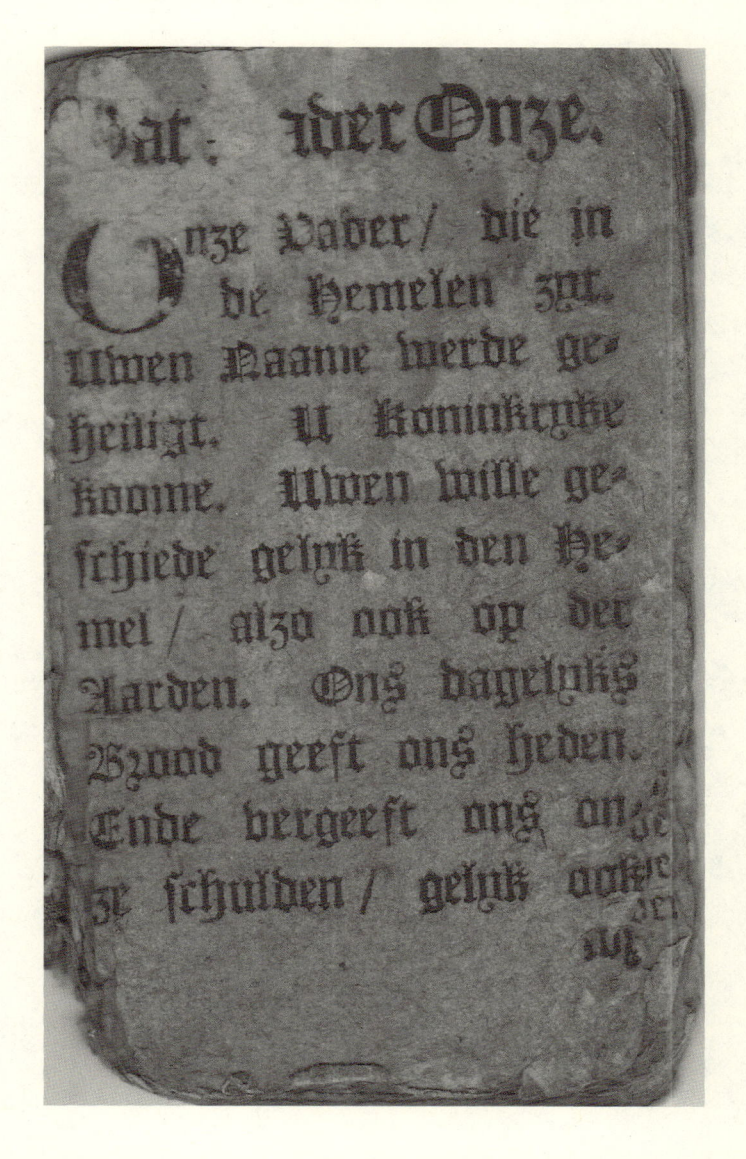

> Vat. der Onze.
>
> Onze Vader / die in
> de Hemelen zyt.
> Uwen Naame werde ge-
> heiligt. U Koninkryke
> koome. Uwen wille ge-
> schiede gelyk in den He-
> mel / alzo ook op der
> Aarden. Ons dagelyks
> Brood geeft ons heden.
> Ende vergeeft ons onze
> ze schulden / gelyk ook
> der
> wy

The Lord's Prayer as it was printed in Trui's "Haneboek" (Rooster Book)
the little primer from which she taught the beginners in her classes

Ge Verhoog

Scanned from original documents in
possession of Trui Straatman's descendants.

The cover illustration of the "Haneboek"

The Flowering Almond Rod

"The children will never have to say they did not learn how to pray." This is her response when parents ask her how their children should pray. The book has proven useful for generations of young readers. On the cover, a rooster perches beside an old-fashioned schoolhouse, alerting the pupils, "Children, learn your lessons well. Roosters rise early, and so should you if you are to succeed."

Trui knows the book from A to Z. It is her guide as she patiently teaches the letters and the sounds they stand for. Some children learn more quickly than others, and some are older – their ages range from four to fourteen. The advanced students help the beginners. Three days a week they learn new letters and words, practicing diligently. By springtime they can fluently rattle off the Lord's Prayer and the Ten Commandments. Trui expects them to sing enthusiastically the songs learned to the accompaniment of the harmonium. She praises them when they remember well.

The parents hear from their children the details of what happens from day to day. They begin to realize that her methods work. They never imagined how this could be, that an ordinary farmer's widow could accomplish such results. Trui must be a special person.

"I had to stand in the corner," one disgruntled boy complained after school.

"You must have deserved it," replied his parents. They know Trui does not punish without reason. "If you dare to be disobedient again, you will be punished at home too." The parents are convinced that their baptismal promises are now being fulfilled, and on a practical note, the children are kept busy during the slack season on the farms. Trui does not expect payment for teaching, but many parents feel this is not fair to her, for they know she is poor. Some send three cents every week with their offspring, while others donate apples, buckwheat, or perhaps a jar of syrup.

As Trui watches the children dash outside to eat their lunches, her heart swells with thankfulness. In this country, schools are in short supply and attendance is not enforced. Many parents, even the strictly religious ones, fail to send their children to school. Many preachers shout and rave about Hell and damnation but do not lead their flocks to the wells of living water. "As long as I am able," she tells herself, "I will do what I can to show them the way to the water of life and give them the means to reach it. And who will stop me?"

CHAPTER FOUR

Harskamp Families

Jan van de Pol sits near his smoky old stove and watches Trui, Jan Heebink's widow, as she walks by. He bends forward in his creaky cane chair to peer through the small grimy panes of his window. She has a firm step and an energetic manner. Her long black skirt flaps around her sparse figure, and her striped apron flutters in the wind. A bit of graying hair escapes her ruffled bonnet, softening her appearance. A shopping basket hangs on her arm, and she carries her black woolen shawl.

If I were a betting man, he thinks, I'd bet she has been out visiting the sick. What a fine woman! She isn't bossy or a know-it-all. No, she has a mind of her own and can make a humorous remark at the right time. She looks after her own house capably and still has time for school, the sick, and the foster children who live with families here and there. She makes sure those foster children are treated well. Yes, a fine woman indeed. Never in all his life has he seen a woman like her. Most women are old and fat at thirty. They sit by the fire in winter or on a chair outside in summer to knit and mend old clothes. But not Trui, muses Pol.

He sighs. He has to tend the fire if he wants to make a meal and clean up. He has to feed the chickens, gather the eggs, and heave the pump handle for water to make coffee. Again, he sighs deeply. His stooped shoulders and stubbly white beard reveal his age; he is over sixty and the grave is waiting. Life is just a vale of toil and sorrow. Toil, yes; sorrow, not so much. But he is getting older and worries more. It would be so nice if there were someone to care for him in his old age – a woman like Trui, for instance. Cheerful, efficient, ambitious, talkative, but not preachy. Yes, someone like Trui Heebink. But she never stops at his place on her rounds, and he is facing old age alone. As a girl, Trui was a cheerful, lively lass, but Jan Heebink led her to the courthouse to marry before he had a chance. Of course, she is aging as well, maybe ten years younger than Pol, but definitely over fifty. What of it? His eyes light up. She is a widow, free to marry. Should he? Ridiculous, old Jan van de Pol courting. He will have to work up the courage to approach Trui. Her family includes children, in-laws, and grandchildren. He slaps the armrest of his chair – one minute you're lonely, and the next a grandfather. One minute you dread making your own coffee, and the next you have a good housewife to do it for you in your old age. He moves his chair close to the window to watch for her return. When she approaches in the distance on the sandy path, he

The Flowering Almond Rod

will stand casually in his yard and make conversation as she comes by.

Trui had planned this afternoon for Hiltje, wife of Krelis. They are the parents of Annechien, one of her pupils. She wants to talk about their other children, about sending them to school so they won't grow up as ignorant as heathens — or as heathens? Krelis is deeply conservative about his religion and not sure that schooling is the answer. Trui lifts the iron bar to open the barn door, and from there will find her way into the household. A "clop, clop" sounds in the dim barn, indicating Krelis is at work making wooden shoes.

"Children, go play outside, the weather is nice," he orders.

Fine with me, Trui thinks. Then she can talk with Hiltje and read for her. She passes through the narrow hall, where the sun shines through the brightly colored panes above the seldom-used front door. Oddly combined odors of paint and coco matting meet her. Two painted artworks on bark adorn the walls. Krelis does not like vain exhibits, but one picture shows a woman with hands reaching to Heaven with the word "Pray". The other has a man plowing and the word "Work". Despite her long illness, Hiltje has been able to create the paintings.

Trui opens the door and is welcomed by Hiltje's warm smile. The small rosy spots on her cheeks do not bode well.

"Yes, here I am again." Trui folds her shawl onto a chair and digs into her basket for the eggs and book she has brought. "Conversation isn't always necessary, so I'll read for you today."

Hiltje nods. She already knows Trui's favorite readings, but it doesn't matter – books about one's faith are always welcome. But Trui waits. "How are you now, Hiltje?"

Hiltje smiles faintly. "The Lord will provide," she whispers submissively.

Trui is irritated, but keeps it to herself. "You are giving up. This not the way to get better."

Hiltje coughs weakly. "Get better? You know I never will, Trui."

Trui regards Hiltje, not yet forty years old and dying of tuberculosis. It happens to so many young mothers of busy families. It is a curse in this nation and there is no remedy.

"Krelis met an old friend who claims to have a special cure," Hiltje continues. "He wants me to send the doctor away and try it." She hesitates. "I don't like it at all, but you know Krelis – he makes it so difficult."

Yes, Trui knows Krelis. He knows it all better than everyone. Ten children when Hiltje is so weak. "Now he brings this quack and hands out advice on things about which he knows nothing. If you die, he will say it is the will of God, it had to be that way, there must be a reason." Trui shakes her head.

"That's true, isn't it?" Hiltje is troubled.

"Of course not," snaps Trui. "The doctor is well trained in his profession and knows what he is doing. That friend of Krelis is a fake."

"But sometimes there are miraculous cures."

"Did they happen to you? Some people begin to believe their own lies." Trui straightens her back. "Hiltje, my girl, better say no to that quack."

"If only I could. Krelis is so... so...."

"I don't understand you and Krelis. Your church makes rules for everything. You are seriously ill, but you meekly say it is the will of God. The Bible says 'Pray without ceasing,' so you ought to ask the Lord for help. God wants His children to come to Him when they are in need. Krelis thinks rules and laws are so important, but he disdains the doctor and believes in a quack." She stops suddenly.

Krelis enters. "Hello."

"Good day. We were just talking about you."

Krelis pulls his chair closer. He sits on it backwards, his arms resting on the back. He stares at Trui. "I'm listening."

"If only you would. I heard about your friend with the miracle cures."

"You are so right. He's the only one who can cure my wife."

"How do you know that?"

"I know it because I have seen him pray and draw power from above." He straightens his posture. "We should not put our trust in ordinary men. Wait and see."

"And you have found a new kind of medicine man?"

"He is the only one who should be allowed to tend the sick. Those other doctors just work for money and show.

When we lament to God and He does not answer, we have to submit to our lot. The Lord gives, the Lord takes away."

"But you will be left with ten children."

"Children are a treasure of the Lord. He will take care of them."

To avoid hurting Hiltje, Trui holds her tongue from making a sharp rebuke. What would Krelis answer if she remarked that ten children are more likely a result of his own lust and carelessness? How could it be right for ten children to grow up without a mother? Could it be God's will that a woman suffers and dies before her time, worn out by childbearing? Trui has opinions on this, but knows that to voice them would bring a storm of misunderstanding and controversy. In the end it would do no good.

The room is quiet except for Hiltje's coughing. "We have to bend under the heavy hand of God upon us," Krelis says. "We do that by submitting to His will. Everything happens as it is ordained by the will of God."

Trui thinks about his words. She knows the people of Harskamp – they appear to show an attitude of submissiveness to the consuming fire of God. She sees also a complacent pride in their humility, like a cushioned armchair. It irritates her to no end. Has she not had her share of troubles? Has she not found refuge in her faith during her bitter losses? She shakes her shoulders as if to get rid of Krelis' depressing words.

She accuses, "You act as if God enjoys punishing you with troubles."

Krelis defends himself. "We live under just judgment and wrath. I wish you would see the light. You will not bow down under God's anger, but I tell you, the day will come when He calls mountains to fall upon us and hills to cover us."

Trui packs her book back into her basket, thinking what a strange visit this has been. "Well, I believe in that day we had better not call on the hills and mountains for help, but just turn to Jesus. I read in the Bible that Jesus made us free from all fear and that we are God's children."

Krelis shakes his head over such flighty ideas, but Trui stops the discussion. Hiltje is sick and doesn't need their arguments. "When are the other children coming to school?" She senses Krelis' objections.

"I would like them to go," Hiltje says. "I have said it so often. Annechien loves school."

Krelis sighs deeply. "Trui, I appreciate your ambition, but I don't always agree with you. A woman should stay in her house, not take a path that leads away from home and family. Some of the hymns you teach are not always proper. The psalms are not so bad. The children should learn to plead for grace. You have to point out our lost sinful state, how we, like bending rushes, poor and miserable, run headlong into destruction."

"I'll think about it." Trui is tired of arguing. Perhaps Krelis will be persuaded to send his children to her school, even with its lack of seriousness.

"You would understand better if you were truly converted. You would realize what I mean." Krelis does not notice how tightly Trui's fingers grip the handle of her basket in order to control herself. "I say, with the author of the psalms, about the unconverted who wander about, 'They have ears but hear not, no breath is in them, they are dumb as an ox.'"

Trui turns to Hiltje. "Goodbye, Hiltje. The Lord is with you, and that is enough. Don't worry." As she opens the door to go, she turns to Krelis. "Cattle aren't dumb, you know. Don't fool yourself."

Calmly, she steps outside and takes a deep breath. So that is that. Krelis will never change. Poor Hiltje. She will see to it that the children get to school this winter so there will be less work for Hiltje. She notices with annoyance the broken hinge on the gate into the yard.

"Why don't you fix that gate?" she snaps at Krelis, standing next to it with his hands in his pockets.

"I don't worry about earthly things. The heavenly ones are more important."

"What about your shoemaking business then?"

"Well, I have to do that to keep the hungry mouths of the children filled." He meditates, "But in the meantime, my mind dwells on the bread of life, and I hope you will get a taste of it sometime."

Trui adjusts her basket. "Listen, Krelis, you're sitting in your armchair on the way to Heaven. Be careful you don't fall out. You think you are the only converted and reborn one, but I am glad there are many more. I will thank God the rest of my life for converting me."

Krelis shakes his head. "Trui, Trui, someday you will be sorry for what you've said. I can't understand how you could be born and raised on the Veluwe and yet hold ideas so superficial, so shallow."

Trui looks at him forthrightly. "And I can't understand how you can claim to be a reborn member of God's kingdom with your self-importance and sour attitude. Goodbye."

As she returns along the main street of the little village, she waves at familiar faces in the windows. The children at play greet her cheerily. Glancing at the sun, she calculates she can spare half an hour with the Bouwmans, foster parent to little Eva. Because the little girl's parents neglected her, the authorities placed her in a foster home.

Bouwman does not like the name Eva. "All humanity will remember this name as that of the woman who caused the fall of the race."

Vrouw Bouwman is not as stringent about her religion as her husband. She challenges him mildly, "I know of many people whose names are forgotten."

"Sometimes, vrouw, you talk foolishly; it is sinful to joke about the Bible. As for the child, I will steer her in the right direction. Her name will now be Ida." He nods, pleased with himself. "I like that name. It has the same number of letters, and it's not from the Bible." So Eva becomes Ida.

Bouwman is cleaning up his garden for the winter. He steps over the dry twigs to meet Trui, scrapes his klompen clean on the down-turned rake to avoid dragging mud into the house. "You're here to see our girl? Well, she's a blessing and we're taking good care of her. You know that."

Trui lifts the latch of the barn door to go inside. She knows the Bouwmans, but she is a bit uneasy when Bouwman makes so much of it. In the living room she meets Vrouw Bouwman.

"Come in and have some coffee with us. Bouwman himself is ready for coffee, too." Her open countenance is rosy and her eyes sparkle. A cordial hostess, she serves others willingly. "We're so happy with Ida," she remarks with feeling. "So happy she's not afraid of us anymore." She goes into the kitchen, where Ida is playing.

Ida approaches shyly, hearing a familiar voice. She peeks around the corner and Trui is touched. "Come on here, Ida, you know me from reading lessons." Bravely, Ida comes nearer, her curly hair framing a rosy face.

"Ida has learned to make nice straight lines on her slate," Vrouw Bouwman declares proudly. "I am helping her." Ida returns to her dolls in the kitchen.

The coffee cups steam on the big round table. Bouwman is obviously well off: the shiny wicker chairs, the large linen cabinet, the ornate brass lamp suspended from the ceiling beam. A large glass-framed copy of Bunyan's Christian's Journey to Eternity graces the wall. A row of blue plates sits above the fireplace mantel. Bouwman makes excuses for them – they were inherited from his wife's mother. He wants others to know he is not in favor of vain ostentation, for if they actually became idols, they would spontaneously fall to the floor and smash to pieces.

Vrouw Bouwman asks about the school. Trui answers briefly, for she is not in the habit of discussing the children. There is enough idle talk in the town. Their conversation stops suddenly when they hear Ida singing in the kitchen. The two women listen, fascinated, but Bouwman bangs his fist on the table hard enough to shake the coffeepot.

"Why is that child singing?" His voice is heavy, his eyebrows set in a frown.

Ida sings, "Jesus loves me, yes, Jesus loves me…"

Vrouw Bouwman tries to calm her husband. "Yesterday my sister was here – she teaches in the city. She taught Ida a verse, and it made her so happy.…"

Bouwman interrupts. "Vrouw, let me tell you now and forever that we will allow only pure doctrine. Your sister can talk about love without judgment, but she comes from the big city, the great Babylon, with all its sins and immorality. Watch out for such wickedness."

Trui sets down her coffee cup. "Tell me what you mean, Bouwman," she interjects calmly. "Why can't she sing? I teach the children songs."

"I don't object to psalms, but that worldly instrument – that harmonium – does not belong."

"I use it to keep tune."

Bouwman ignores her. "I repeat, I don't mind psalms, but those ditties about love, that's heresy. Very few people are elected – those big churches have it all wrong. Ida should know only a few will be chosen."

A silence hangs in the room. Vrouw Bouwman wipes her nose nervously. "After all, who really knows? The gospel tells us that Jesus had only twelve disciples."

Trui declares, "I read in the Bible there will be a multitude too great to count."

Bouwman is disgusted. "It's no use talking with women. They think they know the Bible, but they should listen to the men. It is written in the Bible that wives are to listen to their husbands. That is an order."

"Would you like more coffee?" asks his wife. She lifts the coffeepot, but Bouwman gets up.

"I have work to do in the garden. It will soon be dark."

"Oh, yes," she sighs as he closes the door behind him. "Bouwman is a good husband, a dependable man, but he gets too immersed in dogma, and then I let him talk. You can't change his views, but he means well."

Trui drinks her coffee slowly. "I suppose you're right, but they never give up, do they?" Trui thinks of the future. Society is becoming aware of the need for equal rights, but will it ever happen? Would a woman who leaves the drudgery of the washboard and childbearing ever be looked upon as normal? The struggle will be difficult and will never be totally resolved. Men may make some concessions, they may be intrigued by the struggle, they may use women's rights to gain a political edge, but deep down they will always consider themselves the pinnacle of creation. Men...

The Flowering Almond Rod

they'd like to forget that in the Garden of Eden, Adam gave in weakly when Eve urged him to eat the apple.

Trui speaks her mind. "You may gain peace of mind when you don't fight back, but that's not my way. I just can't take the constant put-downs, so I always get into trouble. I can't help it – I won't keep quiet and act as if I agree when I don't."

"But we have a good community of believing Christians here."

Trui looks doubtful. "I'd rather have a church full of joyfully singing Christians. Why should the children of God spend their lives lamenting and moaning with their heads bowed low? Should we be sad when we have eternal life before us?"

Vrouw Bouwman is shocked. "But we have to work out our salvation with fear and trembling." She hesitates. "It's not right to live carelessly."

Trui gazes out at the tall oaks and the distant firs reaching into the darkening sky. "The day I was converted, a load fell from my mind," she recollects. "My questions were answered, and now I want to live for God and do what He wants me to. I'm so thankful."

Her companion ponders. "Yes, but it is not so easy. I worry that my problems seem smaller than my husband's."

Trui rises from her chair, throws her shawl over her shoulders, and takes up her basket. "Think about it. Your man just said that since we women don't know how to understand the Bible, we ought to leave interpretation to the men. They should read further, not stopping at the Old Testament, but continuing into the New Testament. When I read the gospels, I see Golgotha where Christ died for us all: men and women, boys and girls. At any rate, I hope to see that Ida becomes a happy child of God, that's enough." She lifts the iron door latch and steps out.

It has been a busy afternoon, but not more than usual when she makes her visits. Rather than tiring her, the social interaction gives her renewed energy. She looks upward to the clouds. Belief in God raises many questions. She knows she is not without sin, but still she is certain God has called her to be His servant. Whether it is easy or difficult, she must serve in every way she can. It is enough to know God will protect her all her life.

CHAPTER FIVE

VandePol Thinks About Marriage

Jan van de Pol has been sitting at the window for two hours, smoking one pipe after another, and still Trui has not returned. Possibly she took another road home. It will soon be dark, so he cannot work outside or even pretend to. Startled, he suddenly sees her coming. He rubs imaginary dust from his shirt, stumbles to the door, then goes right back in. He almost forgot his pipe. A man can't make casual conversation without a pipe. Trui approaches briskly. He peers from under his heavy brows through the small windowpane as he stuffs his pipe. Now to strike a match, light his pipe, and pretend to be relaxing after working outside. Too bad it is too cold to sit outside on the bench. That would make his plan easier. Passersby always take time to talk with someone sitting on a bench outside. He stumbles into his klompen, trudges through the gravelly yard, and arrives, perfectly timed, at the roadside.

"Good evening, Trui." He acts surprised to see her.

"Good evening to you."

"Nice evening, isn't it?"

She keeps walking without stopping.

He's been sitting there all afternoon waiting for this moment. "Going home?"

Trui stops briefly. "Yes, where else would I be going at this time of the day? I have to make supper. My children will soon be home."

Jan chews on his pipe. Why is this so difficult?

"Have you been out visiting?" What a poor start – as if she's been out partying and he is prying. But on with his plan. He's waited all afternoon, and it's now or never.

"Umm... Trui...."

"What do you want?" Maybe the man needs help, so he should speak up.

"Well, you know, when you hear – I – everything happens as it should – did you ever think about that?"

A faint suspicion comes to mind. The old man could not mean.... She struggles to keep a straight face.

"You are such a busy woman. Can you do all that work by yourself? Don't you sometimes wish for help and support?"

"I can always use help," assures Trui. "I am busy, but I manage all right, don't worry. You just said that everything happens as it should."

In spite of the cold wind, sweat appears on Jan's brow. He doesn't know how to do this. He'd rather plow an acre of land.

"I agree with you, Pol, it is not always easy. According to my children in the city, however, our life is not so difficult.

I've heard that mothers with young children have to work in the factories. It's a pity. Life is much better here."

Jan van de Pol agrees and moves his pipe to the other side of his mouth. "The children should be thankful. In my time, we never had it so good. I remember what happened years ago in Renswolle – not far from here. I was a drayman to Lunteren, where the work went fine. But in Renswolle, the bosses did not pay much, so the workers demanded the right to set their own prices. There was fighting and then they went on strike." He shakes his head. "No, we have it much better here."

Trui looks at him speculatively. "You think we should never fight back? Should we always bow our heads, even for injustice? I don't complain, and neither do you, because we have no reason, but if you saw some of the children in my school and you saw the circumstances where they live, even in our good Harskamp... I ask myself what kind of devilment is going on there."

"Sin is everywhere."

"That may be true," she retorts, "But our government should take responsibility. I accept the fact that God has placed certain people in power, but it's not right for selfish leaders to enjoy expensive houses and live in luxury while the poor go hungry. Little children who should have time to play are working in factories instead."

Pol says no more. Trui is on her hobbyhorse again.

Trui nods, and the ruche of her bonnet nods with her. "I will do my best to tell everyone I meet about a better way.

Some people would like to see women forever enslaved to the washboard, but there is more to life, and that's why I keep visiting. The strugglers must know there is a way out; the sick and the foster children need care."

She steps forward. "In the cities, the daughters of rich men are not allowed out unless a brother or relative goes with them, but the teenage daughters of the poor must work in the factories, where there is no protection for them."

Pol is astonished. He has known Trui for years, but where does she get these ideas? What is she talking about? The big city? What does he know about rich people? He knows only about the rich young ruler in the gospel who was close to the kingdom of God. The factory? He passes them on his freight route with his horses and wagon on the way to Lunteren. But are there children in the factory? He sees children working in the fields in the summer... just a minute....

"Now, Trui, what is wrong with work? Can't the children help with the haying and the harvest? Nobody has ever died of working."

Trui frowns. "Yes, they have. I know this from good sources, and that's why I'll fight against child labor." She gazes down the sandy track and thinks about the sunny grain fields at harvest time. The poor farmer's children have to hoe weeds and tie grain in bundles because there is no money to pay laborers.

"The parents talk piously on Sunday, but when Monday comes, they forget to be pious. They have so many children they've lost count, but that's not a problem, because every child is an unpaid worker." She shakes her head. "No! Children should be in school to study, they should have time to play, and then they can help with chores, but they should not have to work full-time. Recently I was in a town where I saw what happened at a rope factory. They employed children to make ropes outside all day in the rain, the snow, or the hot sunshine. Their mother worked inside the factory, and the babies slept in a corner on rags. It should not be allowed.

"You have never experienced this, nor have I. That is why we are over fifty and still healthy, but those people barely make it to forty. It's because of situations like this that I keep campaigning for improvement. In the first place, I must keep my school going, and I might also teach some adult Bible classes."

Pol's pipe had gone cold, and so had his wish to marry Trui, a good and wise woman, but one who did not know her place. Maybe the school was a good project — at least it kept the children occupied — but all the other causes were just too much. Who does she think she is? The queen of Holland?

"I have to go and light my lamp," he cuts off the conversation. "Time to retire. Goodnight." He lumbers away to his leaning shack.

Trui watches him go. Years of dirt cling to the walls, and the barn is on the verge of collapse. A man living alone doesn't see these things.

Trui heads for home. Suddenly it dawns on her that the conversation took an entirely different turn from what he intended. Does the old man really have intentions for her? Would she be willing if he asked? She must give it some thought. Jan van de Pol – ten years older than herself, not too serious about Christianity. Not a major problem – he is willing to listen. A man could be useful when it came to moving benches and scrubbing floors, even though he groans at the sight of a broom. For years he has transported freight from Harskamp to Lunteren on his big rattling wagon, lanterns on the side. For years she has seen Pol on the wagon seat, bent over, pipe dangling, half asleep, the lines loose in his hand, moving slowly along. His skinny old horse could have traversed the road blindfolded.

She thinks of the day the school inspector arrived, causing her such anxiety. With a man in the house, she could be much more confident. She jerks her shoulders to shake off the thought. She tucks her shawl tighter around her shoulders. Is not the Lord her greatest helper? His help is so amazing; He holds her life in His hands. Why should she look elsewhere?

CHAPTER SIX

Horstman Considers the Status Quo

Herr Horstman studies a law enacted in 1857, carefully perusing the details. Ensconced in his study, his favorite place to spend time, he next checks a report from inspector Limmen. Limmen has brought to his attention a situation that warrants investigation. Yes, the law must be enforced! He lights his pipe. Society is awakening to the need for universal education. Illiteracy augments an undesirable segment of the population. At the same time, the Dutch character is difficult to deal with; Hollanders are a fractious lot. As soon as one comes up with an idea, there is another with an opposing thought, and neither will concede an iota of his position. The government is too divided between factions to accomplish much. Take for example education. In 1806, legislation was proposed to improve the dysfunctional school system. A public school system, neither for nor against religion, would be set up to serve everyone. Universal education would enable all people to function as members of society. The teaching of religion would not be the function of the schools. But what happens? Parents don't want their precious offspring influenced by atheists. They claim there is a huge difference between Christian teachers and those without religion. Outspoken Christian politicians such as Bilderdijk, Da Costa, and van Prinsterer wielded considerable influence over government decisions.

The education law of 1857 was satisfactory, Horstman feels, as he studies the details. The legislators worked to maintain unity but did not guarantee equal rights for all. Public school attendance was not made compulsory. The descendants of those who struggled for freedom of conscience in the Eighty Years' War, however, were not satisfied with the results. The law permitted the establishment of non-public schools, but did not provide funding. Were they expecting too much?

Horstman enjoys the spacious gardens outside his study window. This room, with its paintings, Delft porcelain, thick carpets, and heavy armchairs speaks of prosperity. He thinks of his elegant wife and their servants. The Christians bet on the wrong horse. Very few of them can bask in luxury, for their schools cost them dearly. Throughout the country, they give all they can spare. Their houses are meagerly furnished, the wives do their own cooking and cleaning, and their food is plain. They had to sacrifice, and so will their children, relegating them to the lower classes for generations. In his mind, this is the natural order of society. The rich can have the satisfaction of handing out charity, and the poor will remain grateful, keeping their heads bowed before their benefactors. His wife will retain the right to dismiss servants who displease her — any lowborn scullery maid who dares to be insolent or lazy deserves no better.

The future may hold some challenges, Horstman feels. The poor are not always as meek as they ought to be. The sons of farmers and laborers could possibly attain government seats as a result of this law that permits them to set up their own schools. The public schools cost a great deal as it is. Just look — he shuffles his papers — a headmaster receives four hundred guilders plus a free house and garden, an assistant gets two hundred. Where will it all end? Salaries like that spoil them for life; they are wrapped in silken insulation by the government and even given a pension after forty years of work. Still the Christians insist on their own schools with their teachers living in poverty, but it's their choice.

He blows new clouds of smoke toward the ornate ceiling. Those unlicensed schools will never succeed, but in the meantime, they are a nuisance to the state. Their supporters continue to demand subsidies, because Holland is a so-called Christian nation. They claim, "To be uncommitted is a right, to be Christian is an equal right." The royal family call themselves Christian, but that's no justification for special privileges.

Those who wish to make changes will have a difficult struggle, but those little trouble spots.... Take that old soul somewhere on the Veluwe — what do they call her? Old Trui. She teaches dozens of children who should be going to Otterloo, but their parents prefer to send them to Trui. What irreparable damage she does to the poor children! Singing psalms with a harmonium, memorizing pious little poems, praying like miniature preachers! No arithmetic, etiquette, geography, or biology. As he studies the reports submitted by inspector Limmen, he concludes that he should investigate this school for himself. He dreads it – the poverty, the dirty shacks, the muddy yards, the livestock, the smell – but the responsibility of his position demands it. He will go. It is his work.

The door opens and mevrouw Horstman enters, bearing a silver tray with two cups of coffee. It is their usual evening custom to have coffee together in the office. "Renewed energy for your work," she teases. He nods agreeably, contentedly stirring the fragrant coffee with a silver spoon.

"Did you know that coffee was unknown here a hundred years ago? I remember a friend whose grandfather tasted coffee for the first time and refused to drink it because these modern discoveries would come to nothing."

"People do tend to reject new ideas," suggests his wife.

He looks at her, surprised. "You have a profound thought there in your comely head. I suppose you're right, the Hollander always has to give a new idea some time; he has to sleep on it. It is a good trait, you know, to avoid impulsive actions and wait calmly."

She hands him the daily paper to read. She will read it later, because he is annoyed if he is not the first to read it. Still, she notices an item on the front page:

Domela Nieuwenhuis has stepped down from his position as Lutheran pastor.

The news catches the interest of mijnheer Horstman. "It appears the dominee has had enough of preaching. It may be the first sensible thing he has ever done."

Mevrouw reads further, then asks, "Who is that man? Is he important?"

Mijnheer replies with irritation, "What can I say? A seeker – he is lost and can't find his way, but yet so fanatic he thinks others should follow him. His ideas are not practical...."

She waits. "Well?" she questions.

"You may not understand it, but the man is a radical. He was an honest preacher but strayed from his calling, ahem.... He talks too much about the grievances of the laborers and the rights of the working classes, as if there is such a thing. In fact, this man is a danger to the rest of society; if these ideas spread to the lower classes, they will begin to think they are equal to their betters, and where will it all end? Workers and intellectuals on an equal footing... it would be the end of our ordered society and lead to all kinds of abuse."

He shakes his head, then continues. "That Abraham Kuyper and Schaepman have a lot to say – their Christianity carries more credibility than Domela's, but still...."

"Are they a danger to society too?" Mevrouw is starting to feel rather anxious about the future – she doesn't like dark clouds in her life.

"I don't think so," says mijnheer Horstman. "They espouse a popular Christian philosophy, but I can't understand how such clear thinkers as they are still cling to those old Bible stories. Their preaching, however, keeps the rabble calm. We need rulers to maintain law and order. They probably will keep the workers in their place, not be as radical as Domela would like.... The man even published a pamphlet when he was a Lutheran preacher in Beverwijk on the coast about eight years ago, but it came to nothing in Den Haag on account of his personal problems. His faith was not strong enough to bear the death of his first wife and then the second as well."

Mevrouw claps her hands in dismay. "What are you saying? He has had too much sorrow in life?"

"Ja, indeed. Even though he preaches that God is love, he cannot cope and has lost his position as preacher. I hope it is permanent so that he no longer stirs up the working classes."

Mevrouw cannot really understand. She knows there must be order in society and laws are necessary, since there are some dreadful people who should be restrained. She would rather do her part by taking a pot of nourishing soup to the needy. The poor should be thankful for that and for the worn and outmoded clothing no longer wanted by her and her children. She can sympathize with their troubles, their poverty and their illnesses, and comfort them with a promise to return bringing eggs. Do these people think they can be equal to her, her husband, and others of their class?

Impossible. Should they take part in her social life? Surely not. Should they be educated? She cannot see why.

Her thoughts are written on her face, and her husband smiles. "I hope you understand the folly of these new ideas. Be assured, they will come to nothing. Churches are for the ignorant masses, Domela's ideas for the gullible; we will maintain the upper hand." He wipes away a scornful sneer from his face. "That Domela and old Trui of Harskamp – don't make me laugh! They think they're striving for a better world, but they don't know what they are doing. Like a small spark in a windstorm, they will be blown out before they burn."

Mevrouw stands. "Let's have another cup of coffee. We will drink it without unpleasant talk – we won't spoil the pleasure of good refreshment."

Mijnheer regards her with amusement. She is right – problems are not without solutions. He relegates Trui and Domela, as well as the great Abraham Kuyper, to the side. The ridiculous ideas some people come up with! A good glass of wine will improve his mood. That reminds him of a request from another organization: het Provinciale Vereeniging Het Witte Kruis, the Provincial Society of the White Cross. What a name! They want King William to enact limits to the consumption of alcohol. Utter nonsense! How many liters of genever are consumed in Nederland per year – over fifty million? Ja, that's it – fifty million liters. But to bother the king? Let people decide for themselves. It is not his drink – genever is for factory workers, sailors, and peat diggers. A glass of wine sparkling in candlelight or a prized muscatel goes down much more smoothly.

A request to the king? What impudence! Drinking away their sorrows? Rubbish. Let the workers' children into the factories to earn their few cents so they learn the value of money and stay off the streets as well, keeping out of trouble and away from mischief. Work is useful, and they are never too young to learn. The king has more important things to concern him. Take the yearly budget, for example. There are so many demands; everyone wants a slice. Half a million for elementary education, an astronomical amount for those barely intelligent enough to warrant the cost. Ja, for the children of the upper classes it may be worthwhile. The system works well enough, doesn't it? And salaries are high.

He sighs. It's always those Christian extremists who make trouble. They make life difficult when it could be so peaceful.

But Trui must be stopped. And Domela too.

Resolutely, he takes his second cup of coffee. Obviously a man as well to do as he is has the wisdom and insight to deal with these matters. Fortunately, he is in a position to take control of the situation. Heads will roll.

CHAPTER SEVEN

Life and Death

Trui is quite sure her son Kornelis is courting Evertje. It is better for a grown young man to start his own family than to stay at home with his mother. But he teases her, "Why should I find a wife while I have such a good life here?"

"You know better than that," is her crusty response. They prepare for the wedding. Weddings are contagious, and Jannetje is seeing a young man as well. Gerrit does not think about girls, he claims, but Trui does not believe him.

Trui will be busier than ever now that a new grandchild may soon arrive. She worries about Mina, who is due to give birth. The young family has no money for an expensive doctor, so Trui will perform the duties of a midwife. Her children prefer their mother's help to that of a stranger anyway. When the hour of delivery arrives, the men usually work off their anxiety out in the fields. They think their only responsibility is to initiate the process, while the rest is strictly women's business.

"The Lord will help you through," she tries to calm Mina. She knows her daughter is having as difficult a time as in her previous pregnancy and will never have a large family. Her mother's presence gives Mina confidence; she feels a powerful support in her help, but she envies her faith during this critical hour. When the pain cuts through her, it means life or death, and she calls to God with her whole being.

In her first nine years, Mina had never heard about God, and it is still not clear to her. When Trui accepted Christ, she tried her best to share her faith with her children.

Mina wonders, Do you have to be converted? Do you have to know the date you accepted Christ? She doesn't always understand her mother's Bible talk. Between pains she asks, "Mother, if I should die, if the Lord takes me away...."

Trui wipes the sweat from her brow. "Well, child, I prayed to the Lord to spare you, but if the Lord has other plans for you...." She cannot utter more, for she loves her daughter. "The Lord provides for us in life and death. We are never alone. He has promised, 'Fear not, I am with you.'"

"Maybe the Lord doesn't know me," Mina sighs. "Am I converted, Mother? I don't remember a special date, nor did I ever feel like shouting 'I am saved.' I just don't know."

Trui prays in her heart. "Mina, listen, you don't have to tell the Lord the day and the hour, you only have to say, 'Here I am, I cannot live without you.' That's enough. You don't have to shout hallelujah. If you flee silently to the Lord for shelter, Jesus will be with you." The room is quiet. Trui takes Mina's hand.

The Flowering Almond Rod

"Mother, I could not do without you, your faith is so strong."

That evening the baby cries its first cry, and Trui and Mina are speechless with thanksgiving. "The Lord was with us," Mina whispers. "I know." These have been precious moments to treasure. Soon life goes back to its usual pace. Both know this stressful day has shown them the strength of God's help.

Mina is already up, working busily about the house. Work is the best doctor; idleness is only for the rich. Trui's work here is finished, so she returns to her own chores in her house and barn. The sun casts a golden glow over field and forest. The beauty of the dark evergreens and heather clumps surrounding the little field is better than the finest painting.

As the children arrive for school, the chattering of their high-pitched voices makes her happy. She feels satisfied to have them under her care and to teach them to live as the Creator expects of them. Suddenly a child shouts, "Look, a funeral!" Trui peers over her steel-rimmed spectacles as the procession slowly advances up the road toward them. It must be the young wife of Aaldert Horstweg. She has been ill for months, and now her time has come. Trui makes a decision.

"Come, children, stand quietly in a straight row without talking." With a stern look, she leads them down the gravel path to the road. Nervous and bewildered, the children stare at the procession. Pallbearers in black capes walk ahead of the high-wheeled hay wagon bearing the casket. Trui stands quietly, overwhelmed by the contrast between life and death displayed before her: the sunbathed fields, the leafy trees, the chirping birds, and the young children. Death passes by, real and chilling.

Mina's baby, her newest grandchild, gives her such pleasure as she thrives and grows. Now Trui stands with her pupils, beholding the sad procession of death. The Lord has it all in His hand, and one must always be ready to meet Him. Her life is based on this thought, an assurance that calms her soul.

There is a dull sorrow, a deep depression in the mindset of many in the community. How sad that they doubt their salvation. "We are a sinful generation, and God is provoked. Therefore we must shudder for eternity." They make God into a tyrant who unreasonably accepts the one and leaves another calling in the wilderness, rejected.... As the procession continues on to the cemetery, the bereaved remain in doubt about their beloved's salvation because they read the Bible as law upon law, rule upon rule. Everything must happen as it is foreordained, they reason.

For Trui, the Bible speaks a different language. She is uncomfortable with this passive acceptance. To her it is an unbelieving fatalism, in its deepest sense an insult to God, the loving father, who is not an unmovable judge. Her eyes follow the cluster of black-clad figures, and then she turns

The Flowering Almond Rod

with a deep sigh to the children. "All inside now." The children slip silently inside.

Trui looks around the classroom and feels happy again. It is good to be able to tell people, especially children, about God, who controls life and death and prepare them for life on Earth and in Heaven. What an assignment!

"That was a sad parade, wasn't it?" she remarks, "But it was important for you to see it so we can talk about it. The Bible tells us that everyone must die sometime and stand before the judge of all the earth. Then He will ask us what we have done in our lives, whether good or bad." A sense of awe hangs over the classroom, because the teaching in the homes of the children has been pervaded with fear and trembling.

"The Bible tells us that the Lord will help us if we ask Him, and that is why we can face Him without fear when we die. Remember that Jesus is our friend."

"But I don't want to die," pipes a small voice.

"Dear child, no one wants to die, but someday we will. Let's sing a song." They sing, tentatively at first, then with increasing confidence.

Safe in the arms of Jesus, sweetly my soul shall rest....

When the song ends, a girl raises her hand. "I like the song about the children thronging before the throne of God."

"Then we will sing that one too."

There are no more classes that day – they have enough to think about. As the children scamper away, tears swell in Trui's eyes. That is life, facing even death with a song of praise to God. She will work in God's kingdom with all her energy as long as He finds her worthy.

Slowly she returns inside to move the benches and tidy the room. She does not see the bare furniture, the ugly dark walls, or the squalor of her classroom in a barn, for she is vastly rich, a King's daughter.

CHAPTER EIGHT

Official Notice

The mailman, feeling the importance of his position, removes a large yellow envelope from his bag. He checks it carefully, noting the return address, and with a knowing look, walks up the gravel path to hand it to Trui.

"An important letter for you, Trui. Addressed to you. What is that all about?"

"You are too nosy," she observes as she takes the letter.

He hastens to defend himself. "You might not be aware of it, but a man in my position never gives in to idle curiosity and always maintains confidentiality."

"You had better remember that," she retorts, thinking of the times he has announced from the roadside that one of her children has sent a postcard. This is a sealed letter, however, so she turns it over and over, not hearing the mailman as he chatters on.

"I am very busy right now, and you should be as well. Goodbye." She closes the door, pulls a pin from her hair, and uses it to open the envelope. The letter has a printed heading: "Municipality of Ede." The contents strike like a lightning bolt to her heart. She rubs her eyes, reads it again, and mumbles through the lines.

> It has come to our attention....

Must be from that school inspector on his horse.

> That you, Trui Heebink, without permission or credentials, do teach and keep a school against the law. This activity must cease immediately or a fine will be levied.

Oh, my!

Letter in hand, she stares out the window. She is blind to the trees and fields, sees only the handmade benches in the room beside the barn – her school. She sees the children, hears them recite the Ten Commandments, and imagines their clear voices singing hymns. She feels the joy of listening to them read fluently through their Bible passages. What will happen? Will she have to quit teaching? According to the letter she must pay a fine or close her school. There is no school, Christian or public, in Harskamp, and therefore the children would have to walk all the way to Otterloo. For many families this is not possible. Why hasn't anyone else set up a school in Harskamp? No one has to tell her she is not qualified, she knows that well enough herself, but the parents in the community have baptized their children with the promise to instruct them in the teachings of the Bible or to have them instructed. That is exactly what she has been doing, but now this school inspector, who does not believe in God, is trying to stop her.

The Flowering Almond Rod

Then she smiles. As if an unbeliever can tell her what to do or what not to do when it comes to serving God! She is so deep in thought, it startles her when she hears a voice outside.

"Whoa! Stand still! You'll soon be back in your stall." It is Jan van de Pol. He climbs laboriously down from his wagon, lifts the lid of the box seat, and finds a package.

Trui thinks, You are not a hundred years old yet, as she watches him, so slow and stooped.. Curious, she goes to the door, for he seems to have something for her. She leans out of the upper half of the Dutch door and greets Pol, "Good morning, what are you bringing?"

Pol scans the package in his hand. "It comes all the way from Harderwyk, no, Kootwyk, if I read it correctly. It was at the depot in Lunteren, so I took it along for you." He notices her rosy face and firm stance. She certainly does look good for her age – and she still lives alone!

Trui opens the lower door. "Would you like to come in for a cup of coffee?"

"Of course," he accepts quickly, even though the old horse is anxious to get home. It's hard to refuse a good cup of coffee you don't have to make for yourself. He drops into the creaky armchair and fills his pipe. Ah, contentment!

Trui busies herself crumbling lumps of sugar to add to the cups. "What's going on today? Is it raining packages and letters?"

"Well, my dear, why don't you have a look at what's inside?" is Jan's friendly invitation. How lucky can he be

– a cup of coffee and a peek at the contents of the mysterious package!

Trui removes the string and rolls it into a ball, depositing it into a drawer for later use. The wrapping paper rattles as she pulls out a box with a slip of paper on top.

"Well, well, a letter from Kootwyk, how nice! The small congregation there held a collection for Christian education, and they used the money to buy new slates for my school." She beams with excitement. "And some chalk too and five guilders besides!"

Jan slurps his coffee slowly from the saucer. It has been a rare treat. "My, my, isn't that something. New slates for the school."

Then Trui suddenly remembers that letter from the government. Maybe she can ignore the threat. She didn't have the courage to ask for slates and chalk, but the Lord knew she needed them and provided them. With the Lord's help she will not let her adversaries force her to stop teaching.

She tells Jan about the threatening letter. He pushes back his cap and scratches his head to stimulate his brain. Replacing the cap, he contemplates, "You know Herr Horstman from Ede? He lives in a mansion and has a lot of influence around here. I've heard he and School Inspector Limmen are two of a kind and thick as thieves." After uttering this profound thought, he takes a long draw on his pipe and blows an immense cloud of smoke.

The Flowering Almond Rod

Trui is not going to give up easily. "Let those rich fellows threaten. The Lord is with me and won't let such people succeed."

"They can give you a lot of trouble, though."

"Listen, Jan, I don't expect to go through life on a velvet cushion. They can hamper our work a lot, but God sees it all."

Jan van de Pol enjoys the cozy little room, so different from his shack. He dreads going back to where he has to gather vegetables from the garden, clean off the dirt, peel the potatoes, and cook his meal. You have to work an hour for what you eat in five minutes, and then you have to clean up your dishes afterward. He sighs deeply.

"Don't sigh for me, Jan," Trui snaps. "I am not afraid of either Horstman or the inspector. I'll just wait and see who lasts longest."

"I'm not sighing for you," Jan confesses. "It seems to me no one needs to worry about you. You always get by somehow."

"What about yourself? Aren't you managing well?" she inquires.

He lays his pipe down, then picks it up again. "No, I don't manage well." He works up the courage to confess his loneliness. "Every night I sit all alone and worry. I can't stand it much longer. Trui, what can I do?" He hopes she will take pity on him.

Trui considers deeply. She thinks, He certainly is lonely. This Jan van de Pol will be lying under the heather within a year. She realizes he wants a wife to keep him company, but should she be the one?

Jan stows his pipe in his pocket, ashes and all. "What do you think?" He has told himself he would never marry a clever woman. He wants a wife to cook for him and feed the chickens. But Trui does that as well as all her other activities – her house is tidy – and he likes her anyway.... Everyone has faults, and if she gets too bossy he can always ignore her. He drums the fingers of his rough hands on the table, "Listen, Trui, for a long time I have turned it over in my mind, so I will declare it now. You are alone and I am alone, and we each have our struggles, and two together is much more pleasant than being alone...."

The humor of it bubbles up in her. Jan van de Pol courting her – she is so busy she has never even thought of such a thing. But... it may be nice to have a man around the house – the aroma of pipe smoke, sitting outside together on a summer evening, sharing the warmth of the heater in winter. Jannetje and Gerrit are still at home, but they will soon marry, leaving her to sit alone like other widows. What would she do with all her energy and ideas? Jan van de Pol is not happy living alone, and he needs someone. She could use some help as well, chopping firewood, outdoor chores.... "Well, Jan," she finally decides, "I think I would like to marry you, but I want to talk it over with my children, you know. Besides that, I need to keep doing things the way I always have. I'm not changing my church or my school activities."

The Flowering Almond Rod

"Of course not," Jan responds quickly. "Trui, my dear, you make me very happy. Let me know when you are ready." Here it seemed I had one foot in the grave, he thinks, and now I'm courting!

"Just remember," Trui cuts in, "I'm not so young anymore either, so I'm not moving out of this house or making any big changes in my life."

"Of course, whatever you say. Just let me know when."

Trui stares outside, bemused, her hand grasping the edge of the lower door. What has she done? Was it a wise decision? It will take time to get used to living with someone else, but she will have a man to talk to, and he will have a woman to cook and keep house for him. We're in the world to help each other, after all....

Suddenly she remembers the letter from Ede. Is she seeking a protector? No, Jan van de Pol knows nothing about things like that. It is not his concern, and he doesn't have the intellect to deal with such problems. Correctly reading the addresses of the freight from Harskamp to Lunteren is about his limit. What possessed her to make such a hasty decision? She thinks about Jan Heebink and leans against the door. Jan, Jan Heebink, that was true love. She stares into space until her eyes burn. But life must go on, she can't go back, she must look to the road ahead.

Trui Straatman, age fifty-three, and Jan van de Pol, age sixty-three, were married on September 18, 1880. Trui's children were agreeable to the arrangement, for they had their own lives to live.

CHAPTER NINE

Faith and Superstition

"No, Leemhuis," Trui puts her basket down. "No, what you are doing is not right! You are taking advantage of this foster child."

"Advantage? What are you talking about? I treat Leentje like my own flesh and blood. In fact, even more carefully and lovingly, but a man has to work for his keep!" Vrouw Leenhuis shakes her head and rubs her arms nervously. Leemhuis continues. "Trui, you know what it means to turn over every cent before you spend it."

"You don't have to tell me what poverty is," Trui retorts. "I have to be stingier than any miser. Jan is a good man, but will never earn very much. Don't talk to me about shortage of money. You may have noticed that I never begged, but my children were well cared for and we felt blessed."

"You keep harping on the same old thing," Leemhuis sighs. "I'm going to do some spading in my garden."

"You don't believe the Lord always helps me through."

"Then why doesn't He help us?" Leemhuis sneers.

"Husband, it is sinful to talk like that," warns his wife.

"You don't even ask for God's help," Trui continues. "Your wife is right – it is sinful to say He doesn't help us. If you were honest with yourself, you wouldn't blame God for your problems. You ought to be more humble and ask for forgiveness."

"I will not tolerate being preached at in my own house, and by a woman at that!" He bangs his fist on the shiny carved mahogany table. "I can't stand that pious talk – you are a fanatic, out of your mind!" he shouts. "You don't have both feet on the ground. They should lock you up."

"Leemhuis, calm down," his wife warns him. "I think you are working yourself into such a state you may have to be locked up. Such language!"

"Let him be," Trui replies calmly. "It is better that he speaks his mind instead of bottling it up inside." Then she says to Leenhuis, "You are right to say I am not standing with both feet on the ground if you mean the loose sandy ground of the Veluwe. Actually, I stand on the rock of my faith, which does not move. The Bible tells us not to build on sand but on the firm foundation of the Rock of Christ."

"You are mad!" Leemhuis wipes his brow with a large red handkerchief.

"You know what is strange?" Trui replies. "You can talk all day about your wheat and grass, your sheep and chickens, and the money you make on it. You consider that normal, but when I speak of the caring hand of God and how I am helped by it, you say I am out of my mind."

The Flowering Almond Rod

"You have to maintain a balance," Leemhuis backs off somewhat. "Talking about the Bible every day is not good."

Vrouw Leemhuis interrupts nervously. "Stop quarreling now. It may be bold of me to say it, but I think Trui is right. Besides the Bible, she talks about many things in our lives. She also teaches children to read and write – our Leentje reads so beautifully and will soon be going to school again."

"To school? Not possible. She has to work at tree-planting."

Trui looks outside. Leemhuis does not know real poverty. He has not seen his table surrounded by hungry children who will get only potatoes and rice, rarely accompanied by a scrap of meat. "The Lord will bless this meal, and it will be as good as a feast," she assured them. It is the truth. Her children were always healthy.

But now it is time to think of Leentje, who is well cared for, they claim. For a few months, Leentje had come to school, but in the spring she had to walk to Kootwyk, an hour and fifteen minutes distant, to plant pine seedlings. Too many families required their young children to help earn money in the factories or on the land. "I will have to find another home for Leentje if you continue to force her to work," Trui threatens.

"What is wrong with work?" Leemhuis bursts out. "Does it not say in the Bible that it is good for people to work?"

"You are reading between the lines," Trui retorts. "It is written that children must be brought up to know what is right. They are entrusted to you to be cared for, not to be used as slaves to earn money for you." She shoves her chair back angrily. "Leemhuis, you know as well as I do that she gets up very early to be on time to work in Kootwyk. It's a long walk in all weather – hot sunshine, rain, or wind; it's uphill and down, day after day. You should be ashamed of yourself."

"She is eleven," Leemhuis defends himself.

Trui flares up, "A child of eleven? Leentje needs a home, school, and time to skip rope and play ball with her friends. If you don't hire a man to plant your trees instead of using this child, I will see to it that she gets a better home." Trui is determined to guard poor children who are homeless or misused. This will be looked into.

"I think so, too," Vrouw Leemhuis interjects timidly.

"You women don't know your place! You haven't learned yet that men must make the decisions. Women know nothing about business. You talk nonsense. Go take care of your house and stay where you belong."

Trui stands and picks up her basket. "I'm going. I will see you again, and beware of women who take good care of their families." As she leaves the house through the rear entrance, she notices large crocks and barrels containing preserved vegetables. Wooden lids weighed down by heavy rocks compress the food into the salt liquid. Sausages and slabs of bacon hang from the rafters. Outside, the weeds and mess speak not of poverty but of carelessness and laziness. If he accepted Leentje as a foster child in order to make her work for him, he would have to be stopped.

The sun is sinking low and it is time to go home. The hours have flown by so quickly, she will not be able to visit Hiltje until tomorrow. Jan will soon be home, and Jannetje may have started supper. As she walks home, she notices how poor and simple the houses of Harskamp seem in comparison with the great Leemhuis farmstead. These houses and outbuildings are weathered and worn. A barn with gaping window holes resembles a toothless mouth. Beside it, in contrast, a clothesline of freshly washed linens blowing in the wind seems to cheerfully waft away all cares. Trui is reminded that when you see the dark side of life, you should observe the bright side, too. The people are poor here, but good health and the ability to work are riches enough.

The weather has changed, and a strong wind threatens rain. Trui is glad to be home. The trees bend over and dry leaves swish onto the eaves. The wind picks up speed as darkness falls. Jannetje checks to see that each door is secure.

"Did you fasten all the shutters?" Trui asks.

"Yes, Mother, everything is fine."

Trui takes up her mending, and Jannetje threads her needle. Trui cannot stand the sight of holes in socks – some have more mended area than original sock! The little room is cozy in the lamplight. When the wind rages outside, rattling the shutters, Trui is not sorry to be married again. Her husband is company, but alas, no ray of sunshine. He is often depressed and does a lot of sighing, but she is more concerned with her own troubles. Jannetje, a cheerful girl, gets along fine with Pol. Gerrit is often annoyed with him. Like young men of his age, Gerrit is anxious to find his own way in the world and can't wait to get away from home.

"Listen to that wind!" The storm howls through the trees. "It will probably blow itself out by morning," Trui predicts.

"I hope so," Jan growls. "It will be tough going to Lunteren with my horse and wagon if it doesn't let up."

"Worse for the horse than for you," Trui remarks. "You can sit undercover all the way."

Pol gazes into space. He does not like the eerie windstorms that blow over the Veluwe.

"The wind gets scary when it blows through the trees over the heather. I've seen ghosts like white women flying on broomsticks," says Jannetje.

"Jannetje," Trui scolds, "Stop talking nonsense!"

"Nonsense?" Jan puts in, "That's not nonsense, Trui. You know there are spirits abroad on the Veluwe. Haven't you heard the stories from Kootwyk?"

"You scare yourself with your superstitions. The Kootwykers believe all kinds of weird things. If they see a lantern flicker on the heather, they think it's a phantom."

Pol fills his pipe. "But the light of Klaas Yonker was no lantern. My father and I saw it. A bundle of burning straw followed our wagon, and we raced home in fright."

The Flowering Almond Rod

"What was it?" Jannetje trembles with fear.

"What was it?" Pol goes on. "Klaas Yonker was a difficult child, and when he grew up, he turned bad. He chopped his wife and children to pieces, and when he stood before the judge, he said, 'If I am guilty, you may burn me in a bundle of straw.' He was found guilty, so that's what they did. You can still see that bundle burning in the evening when there is a storm. I remember that awful night driving home with a load of buckwheat when it appeared over the heather...."

Jannetje shudders, glancing at the closed shutters with their small heart-shaped cutouts. The heather is spooky after dark.

"When the war was on," Pol continues, "An officer sporting shiny brass buttons came by. Some of the Kootwykers thought they were pure gold, so they cut the officer's throat and took the buttons." Pol shudders at the story.

Jannetje sits, wide-eyed. "And then?"

"Then they quickly buried the murdered officer. The sand drifted over the spot till it became a knoll, and I have often seen a white form sitting on that very same knoll."

"Did you ever go close?" Trui's eyes hold a mischievous glint as she pretends to be interested. She studies the sock in her hand for more holes to mend.

"What do you think?" Pol tries to hide his fear. "If you only knew what a ghost like that can do.... I heard there was once a teacher who also had to do the work of the undertaker to earn enough to eat. It still wasn't enough, so he went out on the heather on stormy nights to find lost travellers. He struck them on the head and killed them, choosing the biggest men he could find because the undertaker's fee was fifty cents for large bodies, but only ten cents for small ones."

"I don't believe a word of that. Where do you dig up those tales? Poor Jannetje is pale with fright," Trui scolds. "Don't listen to the man. It's all nonsense."

"You don't take those stories seriously enough. If you don't worry, you may find yourself in trouble."

"Jan, those stories come from fearful people who make them bigger with each telling." She gathers up the coffee cups. "It would do you more good to read what is in the Bible."

"But the Bible has many strange stories too," Jannetje puts in. "They fight and murder each other sometimes too."

"Yes, my girl," Trui says calmly, "It will always be that way. People do evil things because they are selfish, but in the Bible you see the hand of God, and I don't see that in the stories of Kootwyk." She removes her apron. "I believe we need a dominie (pastor) for Kootwyk, and it is time for us to have some sleep."

Pol extinguishes his pipe, rises stiffly, and takes a candle to find his way to the outhouse. The light of Jannetje's candle casts huge shadows on the wall as she heads upstairs. "Goodnight," she whispers.

"Goodnight, my dear."

The candle flame flickers suddenly in a draft, causing Jannetje to scream.

"What's the matter, girl?"

"That candle acts so strange. It never did that before, and it is so dark on the ladder."

Trui takes the candle from the girl's shaking hands. "Silly girl. All these years I've taught you never to be frightened, and now Pol with his foolish stories has you screaming like a pig in a trap." She sets the candle down and looks directly at her daughter. "My child, don't ever be afraid of anything. Our God is always near. He will not reproach you if you are afraid, because everyone is afraid sometimes. But you have to pray, and then He will take away your fears and all will be well." She is quiet for a while, then decides, "Let us read the Bible before we go to sleep, shall we? Then we can pray."

Jannetje nods approval. Previously she had no use for her mother's meditations, but now she knows her mother is the strongest spirit in their home... and even in all of Harskamp.

CHAPTER TEN

Second Warning

Once again, the mailman makes his way over the sandy path to Trui's house. He looks at the official envelope in his hand — Trui must have some important connections. It appears to be coming from King Willem III himself. An unusual woman, in his opinion, is Trui. She works hard, looks after her chickens, her goats, and her second husband, but it seems she would rather write letters. She is clever — one doesn't win an argument with her often. Besides that, his precious child, who goes to Trui's school, can already read better than her father. She reads without stumbling, fluent as running water.

Trui accepts the letter at once. It looks important, probably from the Ede municipality or the federal authorities. "You're not going to jail, are you?" The mailman tries to glean some information by being facetious.

"Don't joke about serious matters," Trui warns. "Would you like to know what's in the letter?"

"No, no," he backtracks, suddenly remembering confidentiality is required in his employment. "I just deliver, the contents are none of my business."

"The whole community of Harskamp could be involved with the contents of this letter." With her hairpin, she slits the letter open and skims the lines. She reads aloud, "'Since you chose to ignore the warning previously issued to stop providing unqualified instruction to the children of Harskamp and district, you are hereby required to remit twenty-five guilders within the next two weeks. Further disregard of this order will result in increasingly large fines.' Did you hear that?"

He nods. "I'm not deaf. I heard."

"Twenty-five guilders – I have never had that much money, and now it has to be paid."

"There's no other way. If you don't pay, you go to court." Having the important responsibility of delivering the royal mail, he knows the law. "The case is this, Trui: the authorities have to administer the law. Point one: you are ordered to pay. Point two: you choose whether to pay or not. Point three: the constable comes to your door, takes you to court, and you have to pay another fine. If you continue operating your school, another, and another...." He scratches his head. "What happens then? Well, by then you'll be wise enough to quit."

Trui leans on the lower door. "How many points was that? I believe you were on point four, and point four is:

Trui continues as usual. Children of believing parents need Christian education."

"Be that as it may, when you run into trouble with the law, it is time to stop before they force you. What's wrong with public education anyway?"

Trui persists. "You think and believe a lot of things from the way you talk, but you miss the most important idea. They don't think the study of the Bible is necessary in our Christian land. What a shame!"

"What will you do then?"

Trui considers the letter in her hand. What does she want? "I will continue. I will tell them openly why I operate the school. The money will be provided. We have the goat and the chickens, and the children help a little. I'll just keep going, and you wonder how long? Until Harskamp finally has its own Christian school."

"Here? When a public school is being planned?" He shakes his head. "Take it from me. This will never happen."

Trui frowns deeply. Maybe he is right.... The people will have to fund it themselves because the government will not – Harskamp is too poor. "Well, the government pays your salary," she finishes lamely, "But you could be wrong."

She turns slowly into the house. Twenty-five guilders... and if she continues, more fines to come. Quitting? She stands by the little window, hearing in her mind the voices of the children reciting verses, singing hymns. She remains deep in thought, because it isn't easy to see the way out. Then she rallies, looks at the sky, and prays. "It is your

The Flowering Almond Rod

cause, Lord, for which I stand. How can it go wrong? People may threaten me, and I don't see a solution, but I know it is in your hands and it all belongs to you... please help me."

Herr Horstman, settled at his desk in his fine house in Ede, with a complacent smirk on his face, writes to his friend, Inspector Limmen. The letter is correct in form, punctuation, and grammar, as well as displaying his fine penmanship. The newspapers have already made public the fact that something is being done to curb unlicensed schools such as the one in Harskamp. Maintaining law and order is an important responsibility for men like him.

When Jan van de Pol comes home from work that evening, Trui meekly reveals the incidents of the day and the demand of the fine. His eyes pop wide in shock. "Trui, girl, we just don't have the money. You will have to give up the school." He picks up his pipe to steady his nerves. "Trui, this brings the law to the door! This goes too far! What are you going to do?"

Trui's mouth is set in a firm line. "What am I going to do? The same as I have always done. They are just ordinary men."

Back at the post office, the letter carrier cannot keep the news to himself. By evening all of Harskamp knows that Trui has to pay the fine or go to jail, and the children will have to walk the distance to the public school, because Trui has quit.

By the next day, twenty-five guilders have been collected in the community, and the fine has been paid in full. Trui meets the children at school as if nothing has happened. "We must continue," she instructs them cheerfully. "Turn to the next page please."

Some days later, mijnheer Horstman has a hard time believing his eyes as he reads, "Jacoba Straatman, wife of Jan van de Pol, resident of Harskamp, paid a fine of twenty-five guilders on the due date." Even worse is the next line: "The aforementioned person continues to operate an unlicensed school in Harskamp and has no intention to cease." A devilish anger stirs within him. Who does she think she is? Does she really mean to defy him, Herr Horstman, an official in charge of education for the district? There are laws in the state of the Netherlands, and we will maintain them. He will see to it, and he will not be ignored by fanatic fools. Not now, not ever! He writes more letters, seals them, and stamps them for mailing. Christian education indeed! The height of foolishness!

CHAPTER ELEVEN

A Dominee in Kootwyk

In recent years, conditions have deteriorated in the Kootwyk region. The loose white sand forms into dunes, isolating the towns. Travellers using the newly opened Hollandse IJzeren Spoorweg (Holland Railway) traversing the Veluwe toward Zwolle peer through tightly closed windows to see barren stretches of dry white sand. The area suffers persistent dust storms, during which the wind screams and howls in a devilish dance. In a dust storm, a traveller on foot can easily lose his sense of direction.

The powers of the underworld seem to have free play in this region, fuelling the local legends. City-dwellers in the region have rational explanations. They know spooks and hauntings are only figments of superstitious imaginations. The true Veluwer may agree outwardly, but meanwhile he shudders fearfully.

Did not an important man from Nykerk make the mistake of mocking the fears of the Veluwers? He risked a walk through the district just to observe the phenomenon. The sun shone a friendly welcome above. He walked along swinging his cane, a cigar in his mouth and a sandwich in his pocket. He knew his way, he thought; he had no fear of the ghosts of the Veluwe. For hours he walked, but when night fell he had to admit he was lost. Through the whole long night it seemed as if ghosts frolicked around him in the trees and bushes and over the dark heather. Mysterious little lights and occasional screams played here and there. It was a night he would never forget. Never was the first crowing of a rooster more welcome than in that early dawn. Where there was a rooster there must be people. To his surprise, it was his own rooster, for he had circled round to his own home in his terrified wandering. The rooster did not end up in the soup pot like most roosters, but died peacefully of old age, so grateful was his master to hear him crowing on that fateful morning.

The landowners want to prevent the soil from drifting, but what can they do? Planting seedling pine trees might work. This is work for children, as it may not be cost-effective. A moderate storm may bury the seedlings, so what would be the use? Possibly a storm might bury the whole village of Kootwyk.

    The place was called "Cotevick" long ago when they built the church with the truncated steeple, a tower like a mutilated arm grasping above the trees. After some shepherds dug a well, it became a gathering place to exchange news while watering the sheep. Early in the 19th century, the tower was declared a hazard and demolished. They built

The Flowering Almond Rod

a school with the scavenged lumber. A teacher was well paid at one hundred guilders per year, in addition to twice-weekly meals at farm homes. In addition, he could earn twelve guilders for funeral and church service duties.

Kootwyk had been without a preacher for several years. In the past, some famous preachers had served in the village, but since 1868 none was willing to suffer the privations of the impoverished community. An evangelist, more farmer than preacher, did what he could, but it took the inner conviction of the believers to keep their faith strong. Throughout the country, churches were torn by clashing opinions and hot debates as they moved toward secession in the Protestant churches of Holland.

A young seminarian, Jan Houtzagers, caught the attention of the community when invited to preach in the little church of Kootwyk. Not many dwellers in Harskamp had heard of him, but many of them undertake the long walk to listen to him speak. It is November 1884, and every seat in the little church is taken. A hushed silence falls as the tall, thin young man with a calm face and piercing eyes steps up to the pulpit.

"Did you notice how he became more and more passionate as he spoke?" the people ask each other after the service as they gather under the trees before they go for their Sunday coffee. "He is studious and would be good for our church." The consistory thinks so too, and without delay ask if he is interested in serving the Kootwijk congregation.

Jan Houtzagers is in a difficult position. He has chosen to follow the teachings of the powerful statesman Abraham Kuyper, and as a result has been alienated from the state church. Students at the upstart Vrije Universiteit (Free University) are barred from the pulpit, but open church doors and a comfortable salary await graduates of the Stedelijke Universiteit (State University). Many choose to have no leadership rather than follow the Kuyper movement.

"I would be very happy to come to Kootwijk," Jan Houtzagers responds, realizing the consequences of his choice. Kootwijk has little to offer – no state support means the impoverished village must raise his entire living on its own.

He smiles when he receives the call letter inviting him to undertake the ministry in Kootwijk, for he is eager to take on the challenge. This community needs him, this humble, brave little community of Kootwijk. He cannot expect a regular salary, since the people have to scrape together their stuivers (five cents) and pennies. Poverty will be his lot. The struggle with the governing bodies of the church also looms – they will not give in easily.

On a Tuesday not long after Jan Houtzager's response, a carriage from Barneveld enters the quiet little village of Kootwijk. Can this bode well for the peace of mind of its inhabitants?

The Flowering Almond Rod

The carriage wheels rattle over the cobblestones, sink into the sand, and then come to rest in the village square. A tall middle-aged passenger disembarks and speaks briefly to the coachman. The coachman nods, climbs back onto the coach, and settles, hat over his eyes, for a long wait. It appears the stranger plans a lengthy stay; he casts a haughty eye at his surroundings. His gray beard, his heavy buttoned-up coat, and his pinched expression as if smelling something rotten give an impression of utter self-satisfaction.

Curious villagers ask, "Who is that man?" but the stranger does not deign to inform them.

"He wears a very high hat," remark the women. But the men coming out of their houses and in from the fields merely shrug, not impressed.

"Do you think there is anything besides sand under that hat?" The women, still suspicious, try to elicit the aim of his visit.

He merely responds, "I want to speak with the church council." He stubbornly refuses to identify himself and must be content to wait uncomfortably on the rough bench of the village square, since none are willing to invite an unidentified stranger into their homes.

Finally the elders of the church gather after returning from the fields. "You are planning to call a dominee?" the stranger questions them.

They nod.

"Who?"

The elders, in silent agreement with one another, respond, "You already know, mijnheer."

The stranger regards them. Stubborn peasants, he thinks, ignorant but difficult to work with.

"Why are you here?"

The man sits calmly, toying with his cane. "Look, my friends," he begins, studying the silver knob of his cane, "The welfare of this village is in our hearts...."

"And who is this 'we'?"

He shrugs. "That matters not. I have heard rumors about your calling a certain Jan Houtzagers." "Candidate for the ministry Houtzagers, you mean."

"All right, candidate Houtzagers, then. A young student who wants to preach here. I have undertaken a long and difficult journey to warn you about a man who will bring you nothing but worry and difficulty."

There is a shocked silence. Finally, a council member speaks. "Are you not being somewhat hasty with your warning, sir? We don't have a preacher yet."

"But surely you make plans...."

"Ja," they all nod, and one speaks. "Would you, sir, please refrain from repeating idle gossip and tell us who you are and what you want?"

He regards them sternly. "I have this to say: if you accept this Houtzagers as your dominee, you can, in the first place, raise all the money for his salary by yourselves. In the second, you can expect numerous obstacles, and in the third, you will be promoting schism within the church. In the—"

One of the men steps forward, a menacing look on his bearded countenance. "In the fourth place, I warn you for your personal safety to step into your carriage and be gone. Your advice means nothing to us – we handle our own affairs, we do."

The stranger begins to feel uneasy amidst the muttering that ensues – these ignorant people can be difficult.

"I came here for your benefit," he attempts once more to win their favor, but the Kootwijkers have heard enough.

"Listen now, we live here on this sandy land, but we haven't been buried in the sand yet. We tend to our own fires, and those who get too close may be burned. Go now. You don't want Houtzagers to serve as dominee here, but he will come anyway, for God is on our side and he has more power than your synod or your classis."

"MY synod? MY classis?" the stranger asks, but they are not deceived.

"By my lights, no one but a preacher acts like that! Deny it if you dare! This is what we have to say to you: you are the one in the clutches of Satan, and if the church directs your actions, you would do well to break away! Have you ever considered that? Now be gone before we need to help you on your way."

The man clutches his cane as the elders circle him, grimly escorting him toward his carriage. The coachman suddenly wakes up, jumps to open the door, cracks his whip, and urges the horses away with a clatter of hooves on the cobblestones.

The Kootwijkers watch the carriage grow small in the distance and wait till the dust of the road dies down.

"So... that was that," says one.

"I don't think we are finished yet," another comments. "I have a strange feeling in my stomach."

"Still, we will see to it that Houtzagers becomes our dominee. We obey God rather than arrogant officials."

The stranger, indeed an ordained minister, is determined to prevent this young upstart from being called to preach. He is furious that such theologically illiterate people, who should keep silent in the church, do not heed their leaders and oppose those in authority over them. The church's leaders must uphold their traditions and statutes and repress rebellion among the laity – such upheaval cannot be tolerated. They may be bold enough to collect adequate funds to hire the man... that Abraham Kuyper has gained too much power.

He peers out of the little carriage window at the passing scenery as they bump along the uneven road. He wonders if they will win – unbearable thought, but what can you do against their growing numbers? The danger is serious. The people of an affronted community led by a preacher with a grievance can fight like lions for their cause, their church, and their souls. And what if they win? He sighs deeply, but he might be overly pessimistic. After all,

Houtzagers' people are well to do, and so are those of his future wife. They will think twice before committing to a life of poverty. Then Kootwijk will be buried in their own sandy soil and danger averted.

The Kootwijkers trudge home in silence. Deep in their hearts they hold the conviction that they want to hear the true gospel preached, and that their chosen candidate will be the one to do so. How can anyone stop them?

CHAPTER TWELVE

Problems Continue

"Think about what you are doing!" Trui addresses her son-in-law. Why do you want to leave your hometown and go out into the wide world?"

Gerrit laughs. "The wide world? I wish it were so. I can just see myself drifting around France or the United States or wherever."

"You are dreaming. How could you afford such travel? Even if you had the money, it would be better spent on the church or school here in Harskamp."

"But you have a school already."

Trui keeps peeling her potatoes. "Yes, I have a school and will manage it as long as I can, but I don't trust those high and mighty officials. They keep trying to stop me." The potato peeling becomes vigorous. "But they will never make me keep quiet about it; I will persist until we have a school with the Bible."

Gerrit regards his mother-in-law thoughtfully. He knows she is not afraid of the coming storm, for he has read about the controversy in the newspaper.

The Flowering Almond Rod

"I just wrote Cornelis a letter," Trui changes the subject. "He sent me a nice card for my birthday, the 22nd of April. You know that date, but I didn't hear anything from you."

"We were busy moving," Gerrit defends himself.

"You are so busy with everyday concerns, but don't forget the most important things. Sometimes I wonder if I'm such a thoughtless mother that my children forget my birthday."

"Mother," Mina interrupts, looking hurt, "Don't say that. You know better, but moving to a new home is not a small thing – packing and loading, driving the wagon a long way to the new place, unloading and sorting – it takes a lot of time.

Trui plunks a potato in the pan. "Yes, I know all about being busy, but I want to remind you that I always put our spiritual and family life first. You have a new job and a new boss, Gerrit, but don't let the evils of the world entice you."

Mina knows her mother is concerned about her children. It will be strange not to be able to stop at the little house on the sandy trail regularly. Her mother's strength so often supported her in difficult times. It was a rare occurrence last winter when Trui was so sick she took to her bed. But she soon got over it, and now is full of energy again.

"Living in a new place doesn't mean we will forget everything we've been taught," Mina maintains. "We will always remember you, so don't you think that is enough?"

"Oh child, it's not me you should think about, it is the Lord and your eternal well-being. I hope the Lord will reveal what is waiting for us."

"My, you are heavy-hearted today, just not your own cheerful self!"

"I have worries of my own, too. I trust in God, but I cannot shout Hallelujah all the time." She sits silently a while. There is not enough money. Pol is a good man but cannot do much work, and because Trui has always taken care of herself, no one, not even the deacons, suspects she has any needs. She thinks of her regular meal – potatoes with lard – then stops. Why is she not trusting in the Lord? She has plenty of potatoes and bacon. What could be more nourishing? She is ashamed, and the Lord must be annoyed – even the potato in her hand is a blessing, but still....

"I confess I was wrong," she admits suddenly. "I am just a foolish old woman, sitting here and worrying. The Lord has always taken care of me, and he will take care of you too. But I will keep praying for you."

The room is very quiet. Mina and Gerrit do not always agree with their mother; she takes things too seriously, but it still is like a ray of sunshine to hear her words of faith, so different from the negative pronouncements of some of the despondent Veluwers. Trui really trusts in the Lord. They feel a strong bond with their mother. No one else has such faith and courage. She knows what happens in the lives of her neighbors but shares only what is good, avoiding petty gossip and idle chatter. She dares to protest against

The Flowering Almond Rod

officious school inspectors and powerful politicians in Ede and Den Haag in a time when women are expected to stay home and keep out of men's business.

Trui changes the subject. "Jannetje is planning to get married."

"To Job van den Ham?" Mina asks, surprised, as they prepare to leave.

Trui carries the potatoes to the sink for a final rinse. "Yes, to Job, and I am happy about it because he is a good boy. I thank the Lord when my children marry well, but it will be strange when my youngest daughter leaves."

"And Gerrit?"

"Ah, Gerrit would rather hang onto Mama's apron strings. It seems he has given up looking."

"You are too good to him," they tease.

Trui waves them off and gathers up the washed potatoes. Too good? What makes them think that? No one is too good.

The mailman trudges toward the house.

"Another letter so soon?"

"No, of course not," he teases, sensing her anxiety.

"I'm not worried. You are the bringer of good news."

The mailman, recognizing his importance, scratches behind his ears. "Trui, you are right as usual, but if you knew what is going on in the world, you would fall right over."

"I don't fall over that easily."

"In Wekerom," the mailman continues, "You know it's less than an hour's walk from here, there is a little school.

Did you know that? No? Well, then you heard it from me. The teacher's name is Zandbergen. He is a guide in the summer, and in the winter he teaches the children when they are done with the fieldwork. It works just fine, the same as your school. And it's been there for a hundred years."

"That teacher must be Methuselah."

He reacts with surprise. "No, that is not his name, but he does a lot for the children – they read and write as well as your pupils."

"No fines for him yet?"

He shrugs. "As far as I know, not yet, but it may come. I hear the officials are getting quite busy."

"What are they doing?"

"They want accredited schools, you know, all the same, all public. But it's not going to work."

Trui nods in agreement. "No, sir, it will not work. In the first place, parents won't send children across the wild sandy heather... especially if the school is not Christian. You understand?"

The mailman understands. "Well, Trui, I have to be on my way – there's more work to do." He hoists his mailbag and leaves. Trui and her school – what will become of them? She has good ideas, but can she maintain the work? His Marie, who goes to Trui's school, studies like a little professor. Maybe a little too pious, but she'll get over it. Too much of the world is not good, but neither is too much religion. Many on his mail route suffer from over-piousness. Trui is smarter than any of them.

The Flowering Almond Rod

Trui wends her way into the schoolroom to prepare for afternoon class, arranging the benches and tidying her few books. As she works she thinks about the future. It would be so nice if she could afford a cow. Would it be possible? Cornelis suggested it, but he and Evertje just had a new baby and have no money to lend. Gerrit and Mina have just moved, so no help can come from them. Her husband Jan will just sigh all the more if she mentions it to him. No, she has to find the means on her own. If the children could pay for their lessons, she could save some money, but the few who pay at all give very little. Some bring her milk or butter, but that does not buy a cow. So she tells herself, You have a goat, a husband, and good children – be content and turn your mind to the things of God.

There's a rumor that the Kootwyk church finally has a dominee. She would be so happy if it were true. She would gladly walk all the way to Kootwyk to hear the gospel preached. Maybe, she ponders, if all goes well and the dominee is willing, something could be done here in Harskamp. First she must make his acquaintance, and if he is enthusiastic as well as serious, he could possibly preach in Harskamp. If she, at her age, can walk to Kootwyk, then a young man could easily come here. But there is no church here. Well then, the barn is roomy and quiet, ideal for a service. Her heart pounds with excitement. So many would be happy if this could happen. She hums a tune. The plan must be worked out carefully, tested with the Bible to be sure it is God's will.

The next day, up the sandy path, the mailman approaches again. Trui meets him. "It's getting to be a habit with you, visiting on company time."

The mailman waves a letter at her. "Here's another one!" As if he's just caught a big fish. "This time, instead of the government, it's from an important office – look at the elegant handwriting. See the fancy swirls in the name?"

"From Herr Horstman." Trui opens it with her hairpin and scans the contents.

"I won't intrude, but from the look on your face, it seems to be good news."

"Do you know Horstman? He comes from Ede, so you might know him."

The mailman pushes his cap back. "Do I know him? He's a prominent and influential man, a member of every society. He receives letters every day, not just one but a whole bundle – important ones too, if I look at the senders. I am not revealing from whom, you understand, but I know a lot. Did he write to you, Trui? My, my...."

"It is a warning. He is sorry to have to impose another fine and another warning. In other words, quit my school, obey the law, be a good housewife, cause no scandal." She puts down the letter, looks over the top of her glasses at the mailman. "What do you know about that? What has HE to do with it?"

"I'm sure he has a lot to do with it. He has the authority to prosecute illegal activities. Ah, woman, be careful.

The Flowering Almond Rod

Before you know it, you will have the law on your doorstep and you'll have to appear in court."

Trui rips the letter into pieces. "Me, afraid of the high and mighty? He is only a human being. What can men do to me? The law of the country? We are a Christian nation, are we not? Have you ever heard about Prince Willem the Silent? How he fought and won our right to have freedom of conscience? I always think about how he showed no favor to any single idea, but allowed for differing opinions. He was wise to give us that freedom. I wish our present king and his government thought the same."

The mailman stands speechless as she turns away. "My, my, Trui is on her hobbyhorse again, but she is right."

CHAPTER THIRTEEN

The Dominee Arrives

Jan Hendrik Houtzagers and Ina Ruysch, married yesterday, stand at the Amsterdam ticket office. Studying the Guide to Holland's Railways, they seek the train that will bring them as close to Kootwyk as possible.

"Two one-way tickets to Assel, please." Ina enjoys watching her tall husband bend down to speak to the man at the wicket.

"One way to Assel? Where is that?"

"Near Kootwyk. No, we're not returning."

"First class?"

"No, third class, please." He looks at Ina. The man judges them to be first-class travellers, but from now on they will go third class to save money. Ina appears happy, her white hat on her dark-blond hair making a charming picture. Jan Houtzagers feels ready for anything.

"Assel will have a short piece of pavement," he predicts while they wait for the train. "The train stops there, we get out and wait beside the track of the famous 'Holland Railway.' Then our real adventure in the middle of nowhere will begin. A farm wagon will be waiting, we'll climb aboard, and we'll ride in style to our new home." His blue eyes twinkle.

She smiles. "You are teasing me."

"It won't be that bad. They wrote that they are expecting us to come."

"I guess there will be a farmer there to meet us, but I am wondering about the wagon." Ina thinks about her father's fine carriage. They had refused all offers to bring them to their new home. They truly want to live like the people they are to serve. As the monstrous train spits and smokes, hissing to a stop, shouting and the clanging of doors herald its arrival. The engineer leans over the door of the cab while the fireman shovels coal into the red mouth of the firebox.

"Fantastic invention," comments a fellow traveller. As they leave Amsterdam, Ina admires the train, its shrill whistles and rough pounding of metal wheels on metal track as they head east. "Just feel the speed we are travelling – a train is the fastest possible mode of transportation." Incredible how the engine pulls all those cars over the rails, so fast she wonders how they can stop in time for the next station.

Jan and Ina feel the excitement of their new life. They recall the happiness of yesterday's wedding celebration, the solemn church ceremony, the good wishes and encouragement for a life that does not promise to be easy. Jan thinks about his school years. His father, a well-to-do citizen of

Utrecht, died when Jan was only twelve. For years Jan had suffered an illness that prevented his writing the entrance exams to the Utrecht university The family moved out of the city to the fresh pine-scented air of Ede and provided Jan with private instruction, enabling him at twenty-one to qualify for entry to the State University in Utrecht. The instruction provided by professor Beets, a stern and humorless teacher, did not satisfy Jan's lifelong desire to serve God as a minister of the gospel. This institution would fit him to serve a liberal pulpit in a state-supported church, a smooth road to an easy life in a modern parsonage. His mother, however, longed to send him to the Vrije Universiteit (Free University) of Amsterdam, soon to be established. He struggled in his mind, unable to decide. The smooth road would be so easy. The other choice, brought about by dissension in the church, would be a life of hardship and difficulty. The conflict would be long and severe, as predicted by Dr. Abraham Kuyper in his book From the Thorn Shall Come Forth a Myrtle Tree. Jan's mother, a woman of deep faith who knew the cares of life, admired the defenders of the "Doliantie," as the dissenters were called. She was happy when Jan chose the orthodox training offered at the Vrije Universiteit and became its first graduate.

Like their chosen pastor, the community of Kootwyk also struggles with enormous difficulties. He realizes the risks they and he have both taken. He is eager to begin, and feels joy in his heart at being accepted for this work.

The Flowering Almond Rod

"What are you thinking about? You seem so far away." Ina touches his arm.

He pulls his mind back to the present. "I was thinking of the years it took to reach this time and place, this trip – a big occasion for our parents."

"The biggest was for your mother," Ina says softly. "If I could be like her... she is a perfect example for the way I'd like to live."

Assel station is near. They take a few small bags down from the rack. "How convenient it is that we sent the heavy luggage ahead!" Ina comments. "It would have been so cumbersome."

"Just a matter of being organized," her husband boasts playfully. "My wife must be pampered."

Ina is glad she thought to send some boxes of groceries ahead in case there was no store nearby. He was not the only organized partner in this venture.

"Look there!" She pulls her husband's sleeve. "That wagon, all decorated with evergreen branches – that must be the wagon to pick us up! What's going to happen?"

Jan stifles a chuckle. "Get used to it. They mean to honor us."

The man in the wagon approaches and begins to speak. His dialect is hard to understand. Noticing their confusion, he tries to speak high Dutch. "Welcome, I mean to say, and with God's help I hope you will be a blessing to the church. I have come to take you into town for your formal welcome. We are so glad you have come, we decorated our wagons with pine branches. Did you notice?"

Soon they bump along the trail to Kootwyk, thinking this must be how it was for the voortrekkers (pioneers) in Transvaal. The horse plods along, its feet stirring up clouds of dust. The muffled clop, clop of the hooves gives rhythm to farmer Dyk's conversation. His pipe dangles from his mouth and the reins hang loose in his hand, for the horse knows they way. He tells them Kootwyk is glad they have come; small wonder, for it has been seventeen years since they last had a dominee. The people will be glad to help out, but they should not expect to be pampered, for the community has very little wealth.

"There's your house," the driver points out as they ride into town. Ina and Jan have already noticed the branches decorating the doorway. A group of children and adults have gathered to meet them. The wagon stops and they climb down in a cloud of dust raised by the scraping of the horse's hooves. The dust is ignored as the people raise their voices in a song of welcome for the new dominee and his wife. The song is beautiful to their ears, in spite of some disharmony. The council chairman steps forward to greet them. His words falter, but his honest, friendly smile warms their hearts. Ds. Jan Houtzagers responds briefly with heartfelt thanks for their welcome, after which everyone returns home.

They enter their new home where Neeltje, the new maid and a girl of fourteen, awaits them. "No, there are no suitcases, no food boxes," she replies to their queries. "Should they have been here?"

"Nothing is here yet?" cries Ina.

"They always send the luggage through to the main station," Neeltje informs them. "It will arrive later for sure."

"My mistake," confesses Jan. "I should have seen to it that there was food in the house." They laugh at their predicament. "Everything was so carefully arranged, and we sent it well ahead of time. Who would know that the Holland Railway would send it to the end of the line?"

Neeltje returns and raps on the door. "Is there anything I can do for you?"

"Yes," Ina replies. "We would like some bread and butter, vegetables, and so on. When the boxes arrive we will have plenty, but right now we have nothing."

"The train will have your stuff soon enough, and for today I will get you some bread." Soon she is back with sandwiches she collected from some families. "This isn't very much because the people don't have much themselves, but you'll manage for today."

"That's plenty – more than enough." Ina is embarrassed. What will they think of her after their first welcome to have to beg for bread? It might be a good story to tell her friends in Amsterdam, but it's not so funny in real life.

"We should have enough until the boxes arrive," Jan assures her. Their first meal in the parsonage is rather strange, but they didn't want to ask Neeltje for more help.

"We'll go to a farm if we're starving," he promises. It will be three days before their boxes arrive.

On their second day, he is needed to conduct a funeral. It is a sad beginning for his church work, but Jan accepts the fact that joy and sorrow each have their turn in life. The old man who died was well regarded because of his humility. He had never dared to declare that he was among the chosen ones of God, remaining in doubt his whole life. When he took sick, he called the doctor, who told him he might die soon. "Well, in that case," he said, "If my soul is saved, all is well." In addition, his wish to die in his own house had been granted.

Still, the congregation sighs and laments for him, because he had lived eighty years knowing the Bible, and they were still not sure if he was saved. Ds. Houtzagers was somewhat familiar with the gloomy mentality of the Veluwe. He knows he must be careful not to hurt their feelings or disappoint them. At the same time, he is eager to tell them about God's grace and mercy and the joy of believing in Him. To the congregation he says, "He was a Christian, he was baptized—"

They interrupt, correcting him. "Dominee, you are still young and have not reached deeper understanding. Someday you will get there. God's grace is not inherited; being baptized only gives one greater responsibility. Who can say they are clean before the Judge of all the earth?"

"But what about Christ's sacrifice on Golgotha?"

"Who can dare approach the holy mountain of God? We are all sinners. You don't understand that we are all worthy of damnation."

Houtzagers remembers a line of an obituary: In the hope of eternal life, carved on a tombstone. Is there any certainty here in his new congregation?

Someone asks, "Did he speak before he died? What were his last words?"

Another replies, "He said, 'I will risk it, for my heart calls out to God.' We know now that he found peace."

They believe that he is safe in Heaven, but yet they live in fear of a righteous judge. Houtzagers has compassion for them in their struggles with their faith. They know God, but lack the comfort of His love. To see Him only as a judge is an incomplete picture. Why don't they study the Bible more and spend less time debating doctrine? A nonbeliever would see nothing desirable in their point of view. His work here will not be easy.

The last words of the deceased provide a slight lifting of the somber pall they cast upon themselves. They admit he must have knocked at Heaven's gate at the last hour, and God would have taken him in. The dominee speaks words of comfort. Some suspect he is too shallow, too young to really grasp the enormity of the struggle of faith, but the man will be in Heaven now, and they wouldn't wish for anything else. Also, they feel relieved to still be alive. They don't reminisce about the deceased, for life is calling and they need their strength.

A big table lies before them, spread with fresh bread, ham, and cheese. Bubbling coffee sends out its fragrance, and even a small drink is offered. Good spirits are restored. Their conversation turns to grain, cows, sheep, and hog prices. The meal is sumptuous because the deceased was well off and had not wanted anyone to leave hungry from his funeral. The leftover plates of sandwiches remind Houtzagers of his empty cupboard – when will his missing boxes arrive?

"We usually sell the leftovers to the people at the funeral. Would you like some too?"

"Certainly," he replies a little too quickly. "Yes, I'd like some." "There's also some rye bread and currant bread."

"Yes, I'll take that too." Overjoyed, Jan takes home three loaves of sliced bread – food for three days. Surely the boxes will arrive by then.

"Ina, my dear, we won't go hungry anymore with all this food. These have been our 'white bread weeks' (a Dutch expression for the first weeks of marriage).

I've learned a lot at this funeral. I was warned about coming here to the Veluwe. What I heard was true, but it is only half of the reality. We can expect many more strange things to happen."

Before long the church papers print a notice saying that Synod has decided to cut off from their membership the congregation and minister of Kootwyk. Unbelievable!

The Flowering Almond Rod

There is only one answer: the Head of the church, JESUS CHRIST, has not signed this declaration.

CHAPTER FOURTEEN

Trial, Turning Point

"I told you this would happen!" van de Pol exclaims. "I warned you often enough. I know you are clever, but it's time for you to mind your house and forget about that school. Now we are in trouble. Soon you'll be in jail, and then Jan Pol in his old age can come to see you there. My bones ache so much, and you know as well as I do that I have one foot in the grave already, and it seems you never think about that. It is always the school, THE SCHOOL!"

Trui plants her hands on her hips, turns a stony glare on him. "So, Pol, never in our married life have I heard such a long speech from you. It stirs me deeply, but all you talk about is yourself and your old age."

"Is that a sin? Aren't my days getting shorter?"

"You just think about yourself. Why don't you quit complaining and do something? Do you hear me whining? I don't have time for that. If you did some work for once, you would have better things to think about."

"You can talk so easily, but you are ten years younger than I. Death is looking through my window."

The Flowering Almond Rod

"Don't be so gloomy. You are inviting death to climb into your window, that's what you're doing. Get your hands out of your sleeves and help me – I married you so we could do our work together."

This is too much. Help Trui? She married me to have help? He was the one who needed help. He takes a long draw on his pipe. This topic is difficult and deep – where is it leading? Better go back to the start of this discussion. "I still think you are bringing a scandal over my old head by bringing the police into the house, having to go to court.... Woman, how dare you?"

The content of the letter that lies on the table before him is the cause of his embarrassment. Trui has been summoned to go to court in Arnhem. A date has been set on which she must defend the charge of unlawfully maintaining a school. She may have another fine to pay. The dark cloud hanging over their future drives Pol to distraction.

Trui is deeply shocked as well, even though she knew it would happen when she defied the order. The day she has been ordered to appear in court looms like a dark mountain. She will put on her best apron and her Sunday shawl to go to this strange place to answer to officials with slippery tongues who look down on you and try to confuse you with long words. She is filled with dread. She is at ease in Harskamp between the children, the sick people, and the rest of the village, but the outside world, with its pomp and pride, disturbs her greatly. She must go, for the cause is urgent. The words of the Bible give her encouragement:

"It shall be given you what you shall speak, for the Spirit will inspire you." She goes with trepidation, but she is still determined to take the difficult path and not stop. Those who oppose her will not do it easily.

Trui arrives in Arnhem and makes her way to the intimidatingly huge building where justice is dispensed. Her stomach churns when her name is called. "Now, Trui," she tells herself, "Don't let those important men rattle you." She is too nervous to answer the questions clearly at first, but then she grasps the reason for her presence and what the men demand from her. They question her motives and want to know what she will do next. As if from another world, the words rain down upon her until suddenly her nervousness disappears and she is back to her own self. Why is she here?

The fog lifts from her mind and she answers in a clear voice. "Your honor, I don't have to answer to anything except that Harskamp needs to have a school, and as long as it doesn't have one, I intend to keep on teaching. The children must not grow up without knowing how to read and write."

"Why don't those children go to Otterloo?"

"That is a public school," Trui argues. "Baptized children belong in a Christian school where the teaching is based on the Bible. When they had their children baptized, the parents promised that they would be instructed in the Bible."

"Is there not a Christian school in Kootwyk?"

The Flowering Almond Rod

"That is a public school – the teacher is merely asked to read the Bible. What would happen if the teacher doesn't care to do it? Nothing. Besides, it is an hour's walk for an adult from Harskamp, much too far for children to travel twice a day. Perhaps it could be done in summer, but it is impossible in winter." She continues resolutely, "I am of the opinion that children have a right to education, and if neither yourself or the government sees fit to provide for a school in Harskamp, I will keep on with the work."

"But Mevrouw, you are not even qualified."

"I am Vrouw van de Pol-Straatman," she corrects him. "Don't call me Mevrouw – I am not that important. As for qualifications, I can read and write, is that not enough?"

"Do you teach history?"

"Of course. Don't you tell your children history? It is useful for everyone. The Bible tells us a nation that does not know its history will perish."

The officials of the court are taken aback. They have underestimated Trui, thinking they could easily outtalk her. Her words make sense, but the law is the law. She cannot be allowed to flout it and continue as before.

"The law demands that you close your school," the judge announces sternly.

"I thought we lived in a free country. Did our forefathers not fight for freedom of conscience for eighty years? Why can't I keep the children from growing up illiterate? Am I doing them harm?"

"It is the qualifications that matter. The certificates—"

"I can read and write. I read widely and share it with the children, so why do I need a certificate? How many parents don't do the same thing at home?"

"That, Mevrouw, is in the family."

"I do it in my own home."

"Yes, but to children of different families—"

"—Who come to my house, where I help them. Is that unlawful? Is that a crime? I do only what is good for them with their parents' blessing."

The judge sighs. It is futile to argue with a woman. The defender, not a lawyer, spends a long time arguing the case for Trui. He contends that since Harskamp has no school, it is irresponsible to let children grow up illiterate in these times of rapid social change. The future holds unlimited potential in the country's growing economy. People will be needed in a variety of occupations, so it is obvious that schooling is essential. In spite of his eloquence, the decision is that Trui is to pay another penalty and must stop teaching.

"That I will not do," she insists, "And the money for the fine will come from somewhere. I will continue until there is a school in Harskamp, I tell you." Her eyes scan the beautifully decorated walls of the massive structure around them. "The government spends a lot of money on buildings that could do with much less. Why is there no money for a school?"

"We will make a note of that," the judge promises. "Whenever the necessity for a school in Harskamp can be proven—"

"—A Christian school," Trui interrupts.

"A public school will be built in Harskamp." The judge continues, "We will see that it happens when permission and funding are arranged."

"But a Christian school?" Trui insists.

"Christian? You mean a private school? The government has no business in that field. If they want a Christian school with certified teachers and a suitable building, the parents will have to pay for it by other means."

Trui wraps her shawl around her shoulders. She has one more thing to say. "So that is how it is in this so-called Christian nation, in what you say is a crucial time in our history? We are entering a great era, people say, and I believe it will be so if we recognize that God rules all things." She faces them, unafraid, and adds, "I know one thing for certain, your honor: the money will come and a school will be built, because I know the Lord rules above all governments."

It is quiet for a while after Trui, a plain farmwoman, leaves, having shown royal courage.

"The court will adjourn for a brief recess," the judge orders.

The future seems dark to Trui as she walks home, deep in thought. One certain thing is that she will bring the entire matter before the throne of God. To keep from giving up, she reminds herself that all things belong to God, and that she is not struggling alone.

She notices a few children playing by the sandy trail in front of her house. Ten-year-old Gys Betselaar runs out to meet her. "I'm coming to school too," he calls. "I'm going to learn to read! I don't have to work in the field anymore, so now I can go to school." His eyes sparkle.

"How nice, my boy," Trui says. "I'm glad you finally are able to come. And whom do I see there? Our Leentje, too."

"I can come to school now," Leentje says softly. "I don't have to plant trees anymore. It was so far to walk." Leemhuis, her foster father, has finally relented.

Van de Pol stands in the doorway, indicating he has something important to say. "The children are anxious to tell you, Trui, that you have a new grandchild. Jannetje thought he would wait another week, but her baby, a son called Willem, was born today."

Leemhuis didn't get time today to prop his stocking feet up on a chair after his daily work was done. He had to listen to Trui's warning about sweet little Leentje, for he did not want her taken away. This evening he puts on his white klompen to go out. His wife wants to know where he is going, but he doesn't bother to tell her. She is a good wife, no doubt about it, but like a typical woman she chatters about things that are nobody's business if he happens to share his plans. This business he plans to undertake is aboveboard, requiring serious decision-making. With grim determination, he heads for his neighbor Bouwman's place. Vrouw Bouwman is out for a walk with little Eva, whom they called Ida after they accepted her as a foster child. This is fine, except that no one will make coffee now.

"You may wonder what brings me here," begins Leemhuis as he removes his klompen and lights his pipe, "But I have been thinking about Vrouw Straatman—"

"Old Trui," Bouwman interjects. "It must be about the school."

"Right you are," Leemhuis agrees. "You must have heard that she had to appear in court today and that there will be another penalty to pay. That's okay for a while, but knowing Trui...." He blows a cloud of blue pipe smoke toward the ceiling.

"She doesn't care what people can do to her," Bouwman says, "And I tell you, she is remarkable. She is alert and clever and finds time to keep a careful watch over the foster children besides teaching and keeping house. It seems as if no power can stop her."

"She will quit as soon as there is a Christian school in Harskamp. All of Harskamp knows that."

Bouwman nods. "Well, she will have to keep it up for a few more years."

Leemhuis pushes his chair closer to the table. "Listen, Bouwman, that's what I came to talk about. If we cannot have a Christian school, why not just a public school?"

Bouwman bangs his fist on the table. "Man, keep such a wicked thought out of your mind! I will not discuss it with you any further until you admit it must be a Christian school."

"I suppose you are right," Leemhuis concedes, "But what will happen next? I am willing to do what is necessary: sit on a committee, pay my share, and so on, but is it a wise idea? I'm afraid we have to decide soon, because they won't let Trui continue, and that's why I came to talk to you. Answer me: do we build a school or don't we?"

Deep silence falls in the kitchen. Finally Bouwman says, "As long as Trui is willing and able to manage, I am hesitant to start building. We know what we have now. Trui's principles are sound and she speaks and acts wisely. If we were to make changes now, we wouldn't know who the next teacher would be. Just think, we could get a stranger from a secular background to instruct our children. How could a blind person lead the blind? An unbelieving teacher in Harskamp? I will never support such an ungodly arrangement."

Leemhuis knocks the ashes from his pipe. "So it is definite then – no unbelieving teacher in Harskamp. But what if we found a sincere Christian to take the position?"

Bouwman sighs deeply. "Your point of view is still entirely secular. I'm beginning to think I escaped a dangerous undertaking. It is far too risky to start a school." He is not as downcast in his faith as some in the community, but his conscience will not let him support an undertaking in which the devil could have his hand.

Leemhuis walks home grumbling to himself. His mission has failed. He blames Bouwman for being confused, for twisting his piety to keep his pocketbook closed. Had his wife been home, he may have had more success. He thinks, I am a religious man too, and it was my idea to either build a school or help Trui in her need, but that seems to be a sin too. He just doesn't understand. One thing is certain – Trui will have to struggle on, paying fines and going to court, until they find a certified Christian teacher, and those people are scarce.

Trui's case has gone public, the papers print reports, and it is even disputed in the lower house of government. Among the elite, some admire the cause for Christian schools and some sneer, but all want to see what will come of it.

Ds. Houtzagers reads about it in the newspaper. He sits longer than usual and rereads the local news until his wife asks, "What's so important to make you forget your coffee?"

Houtzagers lays down the paper. "A lot of things are happening these days. First I hear that Domela Nieuwenhuis has spent half a year in jail because he stood up for the working man." He frowns, deep in thought. "Ina, I think he was a prophet among his people. I believe the times are over when it is acceptable to think God makes the rich wealthy and the poor destined to slave for them. The

Bible says a laborer is worth his wages, not that the worker has to toil to add to the rich man's fortune. Every man has a right to his own life."

Ina tries to understand. She has never lived among working people. She barely knows her own employees, the maid and cleaning woman. Working people keep to their own class in her world. Domela Nieuwenhuis wants a respectable existence for them, which seems to be justified. "Maybe he is right," she suggests carefully, "But maids and workmen should know their place and respect authority."

"I agree, but we must meet them halfway and not treat them as slaves, as is the case for some in this country. It's not right. We need to work for change, but with the understanding that there will be strong resistance from those in power." He thinks of many former friends who use the Bible to serve their notions of self-importance and consider it their right to be served and shown proper respect by those they look down upon. There are so many instances: the manager who overworks his employees, the husband who impregnates his wife every year at the cost of her health, the patriarchal father dominating his grown offspring, the elder brother abusing his younger sister, the minister bullying his congregation.

"Ina, I'm disgusted with this situation! Outrageous, that's what it is! Outrageous!" He rages on. "How can they exalt themselves above others if they know themselves to be sinners who must beg for grace? They forget that Jesus had to die for each of them as well. They call this a Christian nation! A Lutheran minister is defrocked and jailed because he pled for the poor. Like Jesus against the Pharisees – times do not change, not at all. Domela Nieuwenhuis in jail – a black mark on the Christianity of this country, an embarrassment, a shame."

Ina nods approval. She has been trying to understand the mindset of the people in Kootwyk. She begins to realize that things are changing, and there is rebellion brewing.

Her husband agrees with her. "I'm sure we can expect enormous changes. Just remember how many obstacles I had to overcome before I was ordained as a minister. Those obstacles were not biblical, they were just accepted patterns in our society. Think about the women's movement – women don't want to be slaves anymore. The time will come when they can travel alone, when they can even refuse to marry, and no one will criticize them for it." He picks up the paper again and comes upon another article. "Listen to this. It's about a woman from Harskamp, Gertruida Straatman, wife of Jan van de Pol." He reads the whole report about Trui: her school, her work, the penalties imposed on her, and her stubborn resistance. He remarks to his wife, "Now you can understand who creates rebellion. This woman is a hero who strives to provide a Christian education for children who have nothing. That's what she fights for, but what do the education officials do? They try to stop it, nip it in the bud!" He gets up and paces around the room. "Ina, it cries to Heaven! Is there no one to help her? The church should arise to support her. She shows more courage than the entire church."

Ina peruses the news article carefully, and reads that Trui's persistence has even created a division in the Second Chamber of Holland's government. Then she reads that the state church is against her as well. "What were you saying about the future? This woman has original ideas; she is ahead of her time. I respect what she is doing." She thinks of something. "Jan, we should help her."

Ds. Jan Houtzagers stands by the window, but he does not see the old trees in the garden or the little houses of the village – in his mind he sees something different. Then he knows. "Christian schools should be possible. God will bless the talents of His children. If the government will not pay for it, then we must do it ourselves. His children... His people.... Ds. Lutzen Wagenaar will be here tomorrow to visit. I will talk with him about Christian education. God in Heaven," he prays, "Help us, for it is your cause."

The next day, a covered wagon stops at the Kootwyk parsonage. Lutzen Wagenaar climbs down over the clumsy wheel and traces. "Well, well," he greets his friend at the door. "I must say, the trip was much longer than I expected."

"Come in, come in, my wife has the coffee ready." To have a colleague visit makes this a special occasion. The distances are great, even though trains are beginning to reach more isolated places.

"I am happy to hear news from other places," Houtzagers starts the conversation. "I have become a true

The Flowering Almond Rod

Kootwyker now that the distance from Amsterdam and den Haag makes communication difficult, but I try to keep in touch." Lutzen Wagenaar is a welcome guest. Ina enjoys the company, realizing how she misses her former companions from the city.

"I know how isolated you are here." Wagenaar settles himself comfortably in an easy chair. "I heard about your experience with the bread at your first funeral. It seems you are able to adjust and see the humor in spite of the inconvenience. I enjoy hearing your stories – they keep a person at ground level. It is not good to be a preacher with his head in the clouds, trying to tell people how to live while showing no interest in their daily concerns." He praises his hosts' generosity while unaware that the cake with his coffee is a rare treat. "You probably remember that I served a church in Wons, Friesland. They certainly appreciated a dominee there. They gave me a home on top of a knoll they called a terp. Terps were built up in olden times as a place to flee in case of a flood. The people of Wons built the church and dominee's house right on a terp."

"It must have broadened your vision."

"It did that, and it was needed, because the place used to be called Wodanterp, named after the war god. Actually, I had more trouble with the uncrowned king of the village with his fat pocketbook than I ever had with the heathen god Wodan. The glory of olden times is still powerful, if you can call it glory to be a landowner in control over his laborers. It is not easy to deal with forceful, authoritarian men. One of the things that creates conflict, with all its reckless and tragic consequences, is when a strong man is brought low and he or his sons take vengeance...." He strokes his beard and shakes his head. "If you knew the ungodly ways the powerful can act, and you discover how their own pride is much more important than the honor of God's kingdom.... They are totally blind to the gospel when their own honor is at stake."

"Typically Friesian?" Ina asks.

"I don't think so," Wagenaar replies. "Our people are not easygoing. They have had a hard existence wresting their land from the sea. They became skillful dike builders, and learned to be constantly alert for floods. They have developed a special character: hard and tough, never mild, but ready to stand by in need."

Houtzagers thinks about the Veluwe. "Do you think every province of Holland forms its own type of character? The struggles and spiritual conflicts vary from one place to another." "Possibly, but there is one negative trait they all have in common: the narrow-mindedness they get from living in the same place their whole life. The fragmentation within the churches results from this. After I left the church in Wons, they were unable to attract another preacher. They did not want a liberal minister, and none of our friends felt called to go there." There is a slight bitterness in his voice.

"Too bad," Houtzagers observes, "That so few dedicated ministers dare to go to a poor village. I know it is not easy. Money is pleasant to have, but you cannot buy happiness, and we depend more on God than on money in the bank."

Ds. Wagenaar looks around. He can see that his hosts, in spite of coming from well-to-do families, live very simply. "So in Wons, the church simply ceased to have services. However, there was this principal of the Christian school...."

"There was a Christian school?" Houtzagers asks, surprised.

"Certainly. Herr Flor, the headmaster, provided religious instruction every Sunday in his home. I know you agree with me that meeting in small groups is a poor substitute for organized church services, but it is still better than formal gatherings where people are fed stones for bread. Now that I live in the city, I am prepared for the struggle ahead. Pamphlets, speeches, and so on must be ready now that the vineyard of the church cries for help."

"It's a pity that we as churches disgrace ourselves in the sight of the world with our quarrels. Somehow it is a good sign when people fight for the truth, for the faithful preaching of the word of God, but it is too bad when they cannot discuss things in a peaceable way."

"This discussion reminds me of the struggle occurring in Harskamp," Ina Houtzagers interjects. "You might think this is men's work, but Trui of Harskamp is doing her best to maintain a Christian school there."

"Who is this Trui?" Wagenaar wonders. His hosts eagerly inform him about Trui Straatman and her work in Harskamp.

"Then we need to go there," Wagenaar suggests. "A woman like that is another Deborah from the Bible. We have to go and see how we can help her. Can we go this afternoon?"

The Houtzagers both laugh. "It takes an hour and a half to walk there, and it is afternoon already. Maybe we could find a horse and cart to take us in the morning." Plans are made to journey to Harskamp to meet Trui. The weather being fine next morning, they decide to walk. "We have taken longer walks than this when we were students," Houtzagers comments. "That was when we had important matters to discuss." And so they discuss the matter at hand as they stride along, swinging their canes.

"We need Christian schools, but have difficulty paying for them. We considered changing the public school in Kootwykerbroek to a Christian school—"

"I never heard of such a thing!" Wagenaar interrupts.

"It is true. The headmaster opposed the church, but the community is working toward Christian education." He sees a long arduous road ahead and considers it a symbol. "We will need a building, but the usual regulations and inspections are serious obstacles we must deal with."

"Time is on our side," Wagenaar assures him. "I have faith it will happen. Just look around us at the heather and those majestic pine groves. The Creator of this beautiful earth will remember His children who trust in Him. We are often thrown into struggles to strengthen us. What kind of Christians would we be if fried pigeons flew into our mouths? We may have to toil with bent backs in the dry ground, but we will be more thankful for the reward than if there were no struggle."

The heather stretches out toward the horizon, and the clouds build awesome formations in the sky as they approach Harskamp. The small poverty-stricken hamlet would not impress a city dweller from Den Haag.

Soon the two hikers find Trui's house. The upper half of the door is open, so Trui greets the visitors while leaning on the lower panel, a questioning look in her eyes. "From Kootwyk? You must have something worth talking about. Well, that's fine, come on in. The dishes are done, the goat is out, and I will make you some coffee. This is my husband – my children are not here. Sit down, you have had a long walk. What time did you start out?"

Trui's simple cottage has a friendly feeling – the fragrance of coffee perking on the kerosene burner and Trui's plain words make them feel at home. The men observe Trui as she speaks while busying herself to make them comfortable. Her words reveal the keen mind of one who thinks deeply about key issues. She tells them of all that has happened – the setting up of the school, the inspector and the government official from Ede, the fines and the increasing opposition to her work.

"And now what?" Wagenaar asks.

"What do you mean?" Trui replies, worried.

"The future looks grim because they will again order you to stop, the fines will increase beyond your means, the constable will be at your door, or worse...." Wagenaar thinks about his former work in Wons and incidents where the army was sent to oust dissenting preachers from the pulpit.

Trui smiles. "You are concerned about all the troubles these days. I have heard they even brought in the army to keep order. The army! Why? Has the government completely abandoned the Christian faith? Did Willem of Orange fight for freedom of conscience in vain?" She shakes her head. "I shouldn't say anything against the House of Orange. King Willem I was a fine leader who fought for the patriotic Dutch and stimulated the economy, but this king...."

"What are you planning to do now?" Wagenaar wants to know. "We can't change this king and this government."

"Just as usual," Trui answers calmly. "I believe we fought eighty years for freedom of conscience, so we should be free. I am convinced that children should have Christian education, but the government does not agree, and therefore we have a conflict of opinion. However, I will keep doing what I know is right."

"But will they permit you?"

Trui's erect posture echoes her determination. "Let them do what they will. My school will continue as it has until a good Christian school is established to take up the work. The Lord will help me – has He not helped me all my life?"

The discussion continues throughout the day. Ds. Houtzagers promises to hold a meeting in Kootwyk to organize financial help for the school in Harskamp. "When communities help each other, they grow stronger. I think they will be supportive, since church members are in the habit of giving offerings to help each other and will be assured of God's blessing."

Trui still has more on her mind. She hesitates, but they encourage her to speak. "You seem to have more problems, so let us hear about them."

She begins hesitantly, "I have no problem, just a wish. There is no church here in Harskamp and very few people are willing to walk across the heather for more than an hour on Sunday to hear a sermon – even in nice weather. My school has enough benches to seat many people. My wish is to have a dominee come and conduct services occasionally, if that would be possible." She faces the men with a look of hope.

"I certainly will be willing to come," Houtzagers hastens to say. "Which Sunday do you want me to come?"

"I will stop in on my travels, too," Wagenaar promises generously. "I cannot set a date yet since I have meetings and speeches to organize, but when I am nearby I will gladly conduct a service."

Trui claps her hands and smiles with joy. "What else could I ask for? Now everything will be all right! Not only will we have the children, now we will have the parents too." They make plans and arrangements.

The school inspector, the government officials, the court, the Synod – all the clouds troubling her mind have vanished. She sees only the sunshine of God's goodness.

CHAPTER FIFTEEN

A Service in Harskamp

It is easier to make a plan than to carry it out, since a church service is not the same as a school day. A minister needs a pulpit, and the congregation must know when the service begins. The news is spread by the school children and at the market. Much discussion and decision-making happens before the joyful event. Finally the Sunday arrives when Ds. Houtzagers rises early in the morning and journeys toward Harskamp. He has arranged for a colleague to take his pulpit in Kootwyk, while Trui's school is transformed into a church for the day. Jan van de Pol has worked hard to produce additional benches for the occasion. Trui has travelled to the home of a wealthy farmer in Otterloo in search of discarded furniture, hoping to find a suitable lectern. In the dusty attic, she spots an item that might serve the purpose. It appears to be a stand that may at one time have held an enormous family Bible.

"What use would that be to you?" the farmer grumbles.
"It's very dirty."
"Well, do you want it or not?"

Trui examines it closely and finds nothing broken or missing. She nods. "It will do."

"How much do you offer for it?" the farmer asks, rubbing off some dust.

"Excuse me?" Trui is surprised.

"How much are you willing to pay?" he repeats, "Or did you expect to have it for nothing?"

"Of course," Trui responds crisply.

"Good day, then."

"I will send a boy to pick it up tomorrow," says Trui.

"Have him bring the money." "No, because you ought to donate it, that's why." She looks him straight in the face and ties her shawl around her shoulders. "You rich farmers have so much of everything and are still greedy for more. I have travelled a distance to find this lectern and must spend time with soap and water to clean it, but you have no use for it and have even forgotten you have it, and still you want money for it. It will be used to proclaim the word of God by a gifted preacher, and yet you cannot give a small gift for such a purpose. I see how difficult it is for a rich man to enter God's kingdom."

The farmer is momentarily speechless. "Woman, you could stand at that lectern yourself, you don't need a preacher."

"Nonsense," she replies. "Don't be a fool. I need to hear the preaching of the word of God as well as you. I need to hear the true gospel – it is a shame how so many so-called ministers speak empty nonsense. They live in expensive

The Flowering Almond Rod

houses, enjoy a good salary and an easy life, but on Sunday deliver empty, watered-down sermons. They spend no time on Bible study. They let the people forget the great treasure that is the Bible."

"Well, I read my Bible," he offers grudgingly.

"Now that a good preacher like Ds. Houtzagers from Kootwyk plans to come, my house is available, but I need a lectern and you want money for it, while you know very well I can't pay for it. There is plenty of money, but it is in your pockets. You forget that it is just a loan the Lord gives you for which you will eventually have to account to the manager of Heaven."

The farmer feels uneasy. He has never considered there might be a manager in Heaven, although he has a vague fear of God's power. "Oh, all right, take the thing for nothing, then. It may grant me a better place in Heaven."

Trui is furious. "If that's what you think, you may keep your termite-ridden piece of junk. I want no part of a gift given with such a sinful tight-fisted attitude. You think this will earn you a good place in Heaven? You would be lucky to crawl into the lowest corner – and that would not matter either if you could only focus your eyes on Jesus Christ and believe in Him." As she gets ready to leave, she relents and softens her harsh stance. "I will send my son to pick it up. Come to church and see your lectern put to use." She studies the dusty woodwork. "Like you: maybe still good underneath, but covered with grime. There is still time to accept God's grace."

The farmer from Otterloo mutters some angry words at her retreating back but does not speak them to her face. There is something he can't help admiring in her feistiness. Where does she get the courage? She lives in poverty, yet demands nothing for herself. Jan van de Pol is a good sort but earns very little, so she has managed for herself since she was first widowed. As she walks away, her erect posture shows confidence in what she asks of others. She stood her ground before the court and all the officials who opposed her school. Even the learned theologians who visited her were surprised at her knowledge and her practical questions and answers.

He returns to his tidy farmhouse and sees the flowerbeds in bloom, the shutters shining with a thick layer of green paint, and the row of clean milk pails reflecting the sun. His good wife works hard from early morning till late at night. When he sees her at the table with her fresh home-baked bread hugged to her bosom while she slices it with a long knife, while she butters it with her delicious home-churned butter and tops it with cheese from their own farm, he knows she is an ideal farmer's wife. That's all she lives for, her only interest: the cattle, the milk and cheese, the shiny clean equipment. Trui, on the other hand, does take good care of her goat and keeps her house clean, but she is also open-minded, intelligent, and has many interesting ideas. Her greatest passion is for the advancement of the gospel and the church.

The Flowering Almond Rod

    The farmer reflects on the differences between Trui and his wife and feels he is well off. How could he live with someone who turns the world upside down? Still, something makes him think. When he gets around to telling his wife that he has given the old lectern to Trui, she will scold him severely. She will say "How could you do that? If you keep on giving things away, we will soon be as poor as she is and we will end up having to sell the farm. You don't understand the value of money, and if you keep this up we will end up as paupers. My father always told me: Hold onto your money, girl."

Trui sets to work cleaning the lectern. She scrubs and polishes it until the natural color of the wood returns and it becomes again a handsome piece of furniture. She feels a glow of satisfaction when Pol places it at the front of the classroom. She eagerly anticipates the Sunday service, hoping it will turn out so well that it will become a regular event. After all, it is God's business.

    Her happiness is boundless on Sunday morning, when the people stream in from the village and farms around. As Ds. Houtzagers takes his place at the lectern, Bible in hand, it is almost too much for her. She absorbs every word he speaks, she sings the wonderful psalms with joy in her heart, and she prays inwardly, "Thank you, Lord, thank you so much." There is joy in this simple building, just an old barn with bare walls and backless benches, but the surroundings are forgotten because Where two or three are gathered in my name, I am there. The reading of God's word, a clear explanation without lengthy elaborations, a seeking and finding of living water, a church service to nourish seeking hearts. Like a spring of living water, it satisfies thirsty souls. That evening Trui talks with God, trying to find the words to express her thoughts, most of all thinking, Lord, here I am, use me for whatever I can do in your kingdom. That is all I want.

In the evening, as he returns to Kootwyk, Ds. Houtzagers rejoices. This Sunday is a day he will never forget. He remembers his promise to Trui to try to find preachers for the services in Harskamp, and the names of several acquaintances run through his mind. He gazes at the white clouds above the dark pines, the blue sky blending into the heather in the distance. If God wants to use me, here I am, Lord. This is your cause; we work for your honor.

Trui's strength has been renewed. With regained vigor and ambition, she resumes her visits to the sick. Hiltje, suffering from advanced tuberculosis from which she does not expect to recover, looks forward to Trui's weekly visit. Trui arranges to be there when Hiltje's husband Krelis is out delivering the shoes he repairs, so they can talk freely. Trui tells her about the church service and the sermon and reads to her from books she enjoys.

She puts aside the book and begins. "There is more I'd like to tell you. The town of Kootwykerbroek now has a Christian school because Ds. Houtzagers encouraged it. First there was only a public school, and it is still there, but most of the children now attend the Christian school. What do you think of that, Hiltje? Do you think it could happen in Harskamp, too?"

The red spots prominent on Hiltje's thin cheeks and the feverish gleam in her eyes are painful to see – death has laid its hand on this young woman. "Yes, I know for sure it will happen," Hiltje replies quietly, "Because we believe what the Bible says and trust in God."

Trui realizes how tragic it is for her to have a husband like Krelis. He is healthy, with no understanding of the nature of her illness. He insists that God's grace is not for everyone. When he frightens those who are weak in faith with his bizarre ideas, he seems to work as an instrument of the evil one. Trui has tried for years to strengthen Hiltje's faith and counteract the dark shadows of Krelis' notions. Why does he continue to spread doubt in the mind of his ailing wife?

Krelis is annoyed when Trui arranges her visits to avoid him. "You should come when I am home," he says as she meets him returning, just as she is about to leave.

"Why? At least I know I am welcome when you are not here."

Krelis frowns. "Your talk is idle and it bothers my conscience," he announces. "You mislead my wife with false hopes of Heaven. I have to watch out for that."

Trui's face turns red with anger. "You just repeat what other doubters say. You only listen to those with negative ideas and never think for yourself. If you did, you would know those ideas have nothing to do with true faith as the Bible teaches."

Krelis looks beaten at first, but then raises a clenched fist at her. "I am sorry for you, Trui, and I hope you will be free of Satan's grip someday." He stomps into the house, throws off his klompen, and goes to Hiltje. "She is never coming here again," he raves. "I will not have you exposed to her constant sinful talk. Instead of understanding that she should be like I am, with my special revelation, she starts preaching to me – that's what she does!"

Hiltje regards her husband. The red patches on her cheeks glow brightly, but she is quiet. At last she speaks softly. "Let her be. Don't send her away."

Krelis looks long at his wife. He knows she has not long to live, and it frightens him. "Hiltje, dear, my mind struggles so much, when I know you are not yet converted. I wish you would experience it like me and crawl on the ground like a worm before God so that He would give you the freedom to say you are saved."

Hiltje smiles. "I know I am a child of God. I talk and pray with God, and I know I will see Him soon."

"What did you say? Trui's talk makes you think these things are too easy. Who says you are elected? Don't you see the deep gap between you and eternity?"

Hiltje turns away from him. "Lord help me," she prays silently, "Help me with this problem...." A gap between her and God? "Yes, there is a gap, the step from this life into the next, but He is there with everlasting arms."

The Flowering Almond Rod

Krelis has had a bad day. In the evening, while he counts the money he has collected delivering repaired shoes, he suddenly remembers the five guilders he borrowed from Ds. Houtzagers. Oh, it was so easy. The minister had led a service at Trui's house, so Krelis went to the service, although he did not feel at home with all those lighthearted people. However, he was broke because people would rather wear klompen than get their shoes fixed. When his family needed money, he used to borrow from the farmers, but they wanted it back in a week: a difficult business. Then a plan came into his mind seemingly straight from Heaven – he would ask the dominee from Kootwyk for a loan. Krelis came to the service acting burdened, pretended to pay close attention to the sermon, sang like a searching soul. He thought that minister looked too young, like a student who thinks himself a teacher. But he wouldn't say anything to jeopardize his chances, since he wanted his plan to work. He needed to borrow money to take care of his sick wife and ten children. This minister lives far enough away, so he won't be back to collect the loan so soon. Besides that, a minister should not be greedy. Encouraged by his rationalizations, he approaches the minister to discuss the snares of the devil and his own deep understanding of his need to trust in God.

"I am a very devout man, but the world entices me at times and deprives me of the money I need. Five guilders would see me through my difficulties, but Satan has it in his clutches, keeping me from what I ought to have. Please lend me that much until Satan releases it to me."

Houtzagers finds this a strange request and debates in his mind whether the man deserves a hearing. He either has a twisted understanding of the meaning of faith, or he is a fake. He gives Krelis the money, even though he needs it badly himself. Five guilders is a lot of money.

Now Krelis has a problem. He has the money to repay the loan, but can it wait? Maybe he should put it aside in case of emergency and pay it back later. No, he tells himself, don't fall into temptation. The money must be repaid, and he had better go to Kootwyk to hand it over. That's the Lord's will, and one must not resist the Lord. The will of God – who can figure out what it means? Thinking about it makes him feel uneasy, so he starts out on Monday morning for Kootwyk. "Will you be back soon?" Hiltje asks, thinking about the children.

"As soon as possible," Krelis promises, even though he is not sure he will get to Kootwyk. Just outside of Harskamp, his inward struggle begins. In the stillness of the heather, the devil comes straight at him.

"Money in your pocket? And it is going back?"

"Yes," Krelis answers, "I'm paying it back."

The devil has other plans. Krelis stumbles over a tree root and falls straight into his arms. With a scream of fear, he crawls to his feet and looks to see who made him stumble. He sees no one, just the red glow of the sinking sun through the pines. He shouts again, looks to the left and

The Flowering Almond Rod

the right, sees no one, and goes back home. The message is clear. He was stopped along the way in order to prevent him from bringing the money back.

"Hiltje, my dear, I tell you, I was desperate when I borrowed the money, and I had every intention of paying it back. My conscience would not allow anything other. I started out on the long way to Kootwyk, because they say that a man who pays his debts will never be poor. But just as I reached the heather, there I met the devil. He threw me down! Oh, what an encounter that was! I staggered to my feet, and then the Lord told me, 'Do not go to Kootwyk. Go home and keep the money and never listen to that dominee again. He may not be one of the elect, so you don't belong in his church.' So you see how the Lord guided me onto the right path. I wanted to bring the money back, I wanted to follow my conscience, but the Lord prevented me and I have to obey."

Hiltje stares at him, controlling her temper. Does Krelis deceive himself, or is he just plain crooked? She will never be able to convince him of his sin, just as he thinks he cannot convince her of sin. She sighs deeply. Trui, she thinks, if Trui comes next week, she will know what it all means. Krelis, however, should never know she talked about him. Somewhere in her memory there is an expression to fit Krelis: the Lord has strange recruits... and my husband is one of them.

CHAPTER SIXTEEN

The Inspector Returns

The winter of 1890 is long and cold, and many people suffer. Trui is getting older, and she finds it hard to withstand the cold. Van de Pol stays close to the hearth, but Trui still makes the effort to go out. Yesterday while visiting her daughter, she met a sixty-three-year-old acquaintance who was having difficulties with her faith. Trui rebuked her sharply, pointing out that her lack of Bible study was the cause of her doubts. Later, Trui worries that she has been too severe and should have realized that the woman was a searching soul in need of compassion. Yet she thinks, When I see people groping in the dark, stubbornly refusing to see God's hand stretched out to them, I lose my temper. Still, I was too harsh....

"What is bothering you?" Pol sighs with irritation as she fusses about. "Sit down for a while."

Trui opens a drawer to find pen and ink. "I will have no rest until I make right my mistake," she explains. "I was a poor messenger yesterday and must correct what I did. I

The Flowering Almond Rod

did wrong by speaking too harshly and may have turned a woman away from God by the way I talked to her."

Pol looks up, wondering what she thinks she has done. "You have enough troubles of your own without spending your efforts on the problems of others." He admires her skill as she dips her sharp steel pen in the inkwell and carefully shapes the words in her graceful handwriting, producing elaborate curls on the capitals.

"I am writing Jannetje a birthday greeting." She writes:

> Dear beloved daughter,
>
> God's blessings to you on your birthday. I miss you very much even though we saw each other recently. Greet your neighbor for me and tell her I am sorry for speaking so harshly to her rather than reaching out in friendship.
>
> Please tell her I believe she is truly seeking God. This life is a struggle, but God will not leave her alone....

The letter grows long, but Trui feels better now. The Lord will take care of the rest. She wraps up in her shawl to post the letter.

Pol warns her, "Be careful not to catch cold, for what will become of me then?"

Trui smiles, amused. "Well, Jan, it will be me that has a cold, not you, I guess."

He draws on his pipe. "You know what I mean," he grumbles as he watches her from the window. She could be eighteen, such energy in her walk; what a lovely woman.

Returning home, Trui is surprised to see a gentleman approach – none other than the school inspector, mijnheer van Limmen. She is angry. Just as the time nears to open the school again, he shows up. Not again! She meets him at the door.

"Good day, vrouwtje, may I come in? It is a cold day."

She scrutinizes his fine warm coat with its astrakhan collar, his woolen gloves and scarf. Silently she opens the door. "I don't have much time," she remarks stiffly. "It's almost school time." She removes her shawl and straightens the pins holding her gray hair in a bun.

Limmen unbuttons his coat and places his hat on the knob of his cane, which he plants between his knees. "Well, vrouwtje—"

Trui's anger flares. "If you want to speak to me, my name is Vrouw van de Pol."

Limmen's expression stiffens. Who does she think she is? Does she realize to whom she is speaking? "You may remember that I am the school inspector. I was here previously," he begins carefully, irritated by her aggressive attitude.

The Flowering Almond Rod

"I know," she replies calmly. "Why are you here again? And in this cold weather?"

Limmen coughs lightly. "What shall I say? I just walked here. And it was a pleasant stroll from Wekerom up to here."

"You mean from Ede," Trui corrects.

Limmen clears his throat. "I thought I should have a look at Harskamp, my thought became deed, and so I am here. My question is, how are you doing? You closed the school, did you not?"

"You know very well that I kept it going. If you plan to impose another fine, tell me directly."

"All right, directly, if you insist. You still maintain a school regardless of the law?"

"Yes, and I will continue to do so until a proper school is established. Why should the children of Harskamp be deprived of an education? Why do these children have to be illiterate? We need a good school here."

The inspector is becoming angry. This woman has no respect for the authority he represents. Her responses, her bearing, her manners toward him are offensive. She acts like those unbearable suffragettes, women who think they have rights – utter nonsense!

"A Christian school, I suppose," he sneers.

"Yes," Trui nods, "That is the only school in which the children learn not only how to make their way in the world, but also about the disappointments in life and how to deal with them."

"Vrouw van de Pol, don't be ridiculous! The government will not hear of it. A private school is beyond what the budget allows. If one should be planned, it will be a regular public school."

"Then you might as well not bother," Trui responds, "The children of Harskamp will not go there."

"Why not?"

Defiantly she replies, "Because my school will continue, that's why."

Van Limmen is taken aback. "We have ways to stop it."

"The Lord has ways to prevent that."

The man laughs contemptuously. "Oh, you Veluwers are so amusing, so very narrow-minded. Pardon me, but it truly amazes me that you think you can continue to defy the law, the Department of Education, the national government."

"Yes, I think I can. If it is necessary, I will go to den Haag and speak to the king and remind him of his ancestor, who fought and died for freedom of conscience in this country."

For a while it is quiet in the little room. The inspector says at last, "They would not let you near the king."

"Just wait and see."

Something in the eyes of this woman tells him she will not be bullied into submission. His position, personality, and power mean nothing to her. He finally realizes she will go through fire for her convictions. She could put his reputation at risk if she were to appeal to higher authorities.

This annoying woman with her Rooster book and her little school – is it worth the trouble to jeopardize his position? What if he just ignored the entire Harskamp situation? He could just continue to delay any and all action until the problem goes away. It might be the politically smart thing to do. To maintain the impression of having the upper hand, he speaks haughtily, "I presume our discussion has come to an end. I must leave and report on our meeting."

"You had better do that."

"Your school will be stopped."

"That is not your decision to make. This is a Christian school." Her eyes focus on him with a look he imagines like that of a mother lion defending her young.

"If this community tries to build a private school here, they will have a difficult struggle, I can assure you. In the first place, they will never be able to afford it, and second, we will do our best to prevent it." He dons his gloves and hat.

"We will raise every cent ourselves," she replies, unbending. "We will resist all efforts against us because the Lord, who is greater than all you people together, is with us." She closes the door and takes a deep breath. In spite of the uncertain future facing her, she feels a wonderful sense of calm.

"That was rude," Pol grumbles. "You didn't even offer the man a cup of coffee. Now he will have more to complain about."

"I think he would find my coffee too bitter. One thing is certain – we can expect a lot of misery, but I will continue until the first stone is laid for a Christian school."

"You may have to wield the trowel yourself," scoffs Pol.

Thoughtfully, Trui shakes her head. "No, when the first stone is laid I will thank the Lord."

The school inspector spends a few days as a guest at the Horstman home. While he is there, the question regarding Trui becomes the main topic of conversation. "It bothers me that I feel rather powerless when I meet her," confesses mijnheer van Limmen. "I will never admit it to her, you understand, but it can make a case quite difficult."

Mijnheer Horstman gazes thoughtfully from his elegant tall window at the fairyland view of his snow-covered garden. "Those troublesome people," he complains, "Those fanatic, rebellious Christians constantly causing trouble – they won't face reality." He rubs his face as if there were gnats. "Still, as you say, we must be wary of them and handle the situation carefully."

The inspector nods in agreement. "I wonder, will their demands for equal rights ever be considered?"

Horstman looks doubtful. "Hopefully not. It will take time, and meanwhile, we will do everything in our power to prevent it."

Van Limmen agrees. "We have the greater strength with which to maintain our position in the matter. However, in Kootwykerbroek they converted the public school into a Christian school. Very few pupils remain in the public system there."

"Well then, the Harskampers can send their children there."

Van Limmen sighs. He is determined there will be no Christian school in Harskamp and will do his utmost to prevent it from happening. But then he recalls the look in Trui's eyes.... His confidence wavers.

Dominee Houtzagers has often described the success in Kootwykerbroek of establishing a Christian school. He encourages other communities to strive for a similar result. The mills of political action, however, grind so slowly he is becoming weary of the struggle.

After presiding at a meeting of the school board in Kootwykerbroek, he is anxious to return home, despite warnings by the board members of an impending storm. "You could get caught in a thunderstorm – that would be dangerous on the open heather."

He feels tired and depressed but refuses to admit it. Is he just reacting to being overly optimistic? Is he just tired after trying so hard to encourage others to his way of thinking? He just wants to go home. He is not afraid of the weather, the oppressive heat, and the threatening build-up of clouds in the distance. As he trudges along the lonesome road the wind blows up puffs of sand with every step, but he is too deep in thought to notice the leaden color of the sky, the faint shadows gliding over the landscape, the intense quiet that has fallen all around. Not a leaf stirs, not an animal scampers away.

The school, he ponders, what can be done about it? In a mood of despair, he bemoans his struggles with stubborn people, with his own failing health. He thinks about his life as a student at the university and the years it took to finally obtain his preaching license. He thinks about his work in the humble little village of Kootwyk. He loves the quietness of the countryside and the direct, honest people who accept him with open friendliness, but it is challenging to manage on the meager salary they struggle to pay him. He wants to provide a better life for his wife and himself in the future. They are too young to give up hope for a change in their situation.

He thinks about the authorities, who have unlimited power in the ongoing struggle for Christian education. The years go by, and the Christian community is still pushed into the corner. They pay taxes for schools, but no one pays any attention to their needs. What about Trui of Harskamp? Will she be able to continue? Are her teaching methods adequate? She is determined to continue operating her school, but the authorities are doing their utmost to make it impossible for her. He thinks through the incidents leading up to the present situation, step by step, during her fight for existence. He whacks the bushes along the roadside with his cane, taking out his frustration. Is there no help anywhere? Does he have to fight this out all alone? He knows the people expect him to be the man who can find a way to start a school in Harskamp. The church consistory is supportive and talks a great deal about the situation, but does nothing. All across the country churches are at odds with each other, too busy with their doctrinal differences to deal with educational matters.

He recalls a discussion with Dr. Kuyper, who visited a school headmaster, Pieter Vermeulen, who wages a long-standing battle for Christian education. Will he succeed? When plowing on a rocky field, one wonders if it is worth continuing. It is so much easier to accept the status quo: a government-supported public school, a state church, a comfortable house, and a good salary. Why all this trouble and hardship? Why not give up? After all the sacrifices, still nothing happens. With every step forward, two steps back follow. Does the Most High even take notice? Is this how life must be lived? People expect so much of him, and he sees no way out. He is spiritually exhausted and the burden is too much. When will it end? Lord, he prays, it is too much....

A flash of lightning flickers through the trees, a sudden clap of thunder vibrates the heather. A wild wind blows a wall of sand up to the sky, obscuring the sunlight, creating a queer yellow darkness. The trees shake violently, the gale howls and shrieks over the troubled landscape. The lightning and thunder build up to a climax as the sand, scooped up by wind dervishes, whirls in all directions.

Houtzagers, in despair, fears this is the end. The storm is so fierce, no one alone on the heather could survive. He should have listened to the men at the meeting when they warned of the impending storm. Staring wide-eyed at the slashing rain, he cries, "Lord, save me, I perish!" Who could survive such a storm? This must be the end. The end? He recalls wishing for the end just minutes ago. Impulsively he runs, but he finds no road, only darkness. He is lost and alone. He clutches the branch of a low-growing bush. It is as if the despair of the whole world is attacking him.

The earth trembles, the trees groan, and then his fear changes to astonishment and awe. He recalls those who lived through storms in the Bible – of Job, Elijah, and the Apostle John on the isle of Patmos. No one on Earth could show such power as the Lord of creation. Who makes the wind and the heavens do his will? Not governments, not consistories or earthly authorities, for only God, the almighty ruler, has the ultimate power. Humbly, he kneels down and prays. "How could I forget it, Lord, that you are the ruler of Heaven and Earth. I deserve your anger. Father, forgive me." He bows with his hands over his face. He cannot find words, but cries out to God, the only one who is willing and able to help in distress. His courage returns, and he can return to his difficult task, the one he could not face this afternoon, but now can anticipate with a positive attitude.

When he rises the darkness is gone, the air is quiet, and a warm, healing light shines over the beaten landscape. The earth takes a breath. The thunder grumbles away into the distance, and the atmosphere becomes still and fresh.

The Flowering Almond Rod

He splashes through puddles and streams of water. He is eager to reach home, feeling renewed happiness and confidence in his work. He has heard God's voice.

CHAPTER SEVENTEEN

School Planning

"Er is geen stad zo oud, of ze is van hutten gebouwd."
(Even the oldest cities began as huts.)

Trui thinks about the old Dutch saying when her courage falters, since her life's experiences have taught her the truth of it. As she works toward her goals, she has no time to consider retiring. Her husband Jan van de Pol ages by the day, steadily complaining now that he has left his dray business to a younger man. Trui occasionally suffers from flu in the winter, but she recovers and goes on cheerfully, because the Lord has much work for her and she has no time to whine.

Her children are happily married, and the number of grandchildren increases steadily, the youngest appearing in 1891: Gerard and Cornelis, Mina's lively blond twins, who see their grandmother often. She loves to care for them when Mina is busy. Trui is thankful the children need not suffer poverty, but still she worries that the spirit of the age may influence them. New inventions are changing the world, she tells them, but the most important things in life stay the same.

In quiet little Harskamp the changes are not so obvious, but when Trui's children come home for a visit from Ede, excited about trains that seem to fly over rails, she knows the attractions of modern life are coming nearer. They chatter about steam engines that will replace the familiar horse-drawn trams and declare that a new age of history is dawning. They are certain that people must keep up with the times and that they ought to adjust to change because to stand still is to go backward.

Trui is not so gullible that she accepts new inventions without question. In some ways they frighten her, so that she warns her pupils in their lessons about the danger of this world becoming a vanity fair. She expresses her reservations in the letters she writes to her family and friends, and yet she appreciates those new devices that make her life easier.

Sometimes Trui questions her own ambitions. "Am I demanding too much? Am I making an idol of my dream of a school in Harskamp?" she asks her husband. "I am certain it is needed, but it drags on and on. We keep on making plans, but nothing ever happens."

"Of course, of course, it is just your own pride, you and your school," Pol scoffs.

Trui sees red. "You are absolutely wrong! You think I want that school just for my own pride and satisfaction? You are so wrong I don't want to talk to you about it again.

You should know by now that I want it so the children don't grow up like dumb geese who know nothing about the Bible because they can't read or write – that is why I want this school."

"Calm down, don't make such a fuss. You have your school, and they do learn to read."

Trui backs off. Pol is right: she has her school, and it seems this is enough for now. She sees no other way – the Lord doesn't even seem to want more, but it takes her breath away. No school in Harskamp? She must have pushed too much; she will have to back off and rethink her attitude. She bends her head over her mending. How could she have been such a self-righteous creature? She was telling God what to do. Maybe the Lord wants things to remain as they are, and she has dared to question him, putting her own selfish wishes first.

She decides to continue quietly, to bury the hatchet and dig it up only if the school inspector stirs up trouble again. She has not seen him for a long time; perhaps he has decided it is pointless to pursue the matter any further. He can impose more fines, but the farmers will pay them; he can try to intimidate Trui, but he will have to be very alert; he can try to create divisions between the people, but that doesn't work in Harskamp. The people of the Veluwe can be burdened down and have odd ideas about their religion, but they form a solid wall of opposition when their principles are at stake.

The Flowering Almond Rod

While all is peaceful and quiet in the village, Horstman and van Limmen make plans to travel to den Haag, seat of the national government. They enjoy a fast train ride from Utrecht to the capital. The have been holding meetings, making speeches, and working carefully to ensure that no schools will operate without fully qualified teachers. The law as it now stands supports their efforts.

Trui knows the mindset of the farmers on their meagre sandy acres. When she visits their dusty farmsteads with their old sheepcotes and dilapidated barns, when she hears the creak of wagons drawn by slow-moving horses and the barking of chained-up dogs, she knows that, in spite of their struggles, these people will oppose any threat to their freedom of conscience. Repeated warnings have not moved them, and they will not back down when critics threaten to destroy their school. They have collected what money they can spare to help her keep on teaching their children about the Bible. This has given her the security to continue operating the school as long as she is able. She is determined to repay their confidence by doing so.

De heer Horstman rubs his hands together with satisfaction as he travels home from the meeting in den Haag. Van Limmen sits across from him, enjoying the comfortable train trip, feeling equally satisfied with the results of the meeting.

"Those gentlemen den Haag are correct," Horstman opines. "I agree, we should not be so upset by the common people – they will always grumble and think they know all about education. Consider this fine railroad – how they opposed it, what ridiculous objections they raised! The Holland Iron Railway has earned its name both literally and figuratively. The builders persisted, and now everyone is happy with the business and prosperity it brings."

Van Limmen agrees.

Horstman adds, "Too bad we always have to fight every step of the way toward progress because of the competition. Just think of the dispute between the Iron Railway and the Rijnspoorweg – Amsterdam wants the upper hand and they will gain it, I think, since it is a powerful city, but even they may be brought down by the underdogs. So many railway stations in the country have no right to exist and should be eliminated, especially the ones where there is the most opposition. In the end, those rebels will have to submit to the state and the capital," he concludes.

"Those people with their petty objections will always be butting their heads against the established orders," Limmen comments.

Horstman laughs. "Exactly the problem we now deal with – that school is a parallel situation. The protesters must be brought into line and the state given full authority." They discuss plans while the train rattles on in its monotonous rhythm. Den Haag is powerful, and they have an important task in improving education in this blessed land. They have the backing of the government, granting them the power to override anything that hinders progress. Nederland must regain its glory, becoming broadminded, overcoming differences in religion and belief systems. The ideal is to be one people, unified in human values, in a strong economy, a single school system – this is the way to strength and freedom....

Freedom? In the time of the French oppression, a certain Dutchman quietly, in his private study, assembled a constitution for a free new Nederland for a country that was under the heel of Napoleon. He made plans for a free nation, but had to hide his papers from the authorities of that time.

While mijnheer Horstman and the school inspector return from their trip to den Haag, full of their own importance as defenders of the law and champions of the established system of public education, somewhere near Harskamp a simple farmer, Jan Hendrik Bouw, sits night after night, writing in large letters a document of many pages. He wears out many pen nibs and spills ink on Tante Keetje's good tablecloth. She frowns, but he doesn't hear her quietly muttering complaints. He has an important idea and must work it out – he is drafting a constitution for a Christian school in Harskamp, a school that may never come into being, but still....

"I don't know yet," mumbles Bouw when Keetje, his wife, asks him when he will be finished with his scribbling. She shudders with apprehension, realizing her husband is defying the law.

"Before you know it, a constable will be at the door, you'll be jailed as a criminal, and then who will feed and milk the cows?"

Bouw ignores his wife. He feels compelled to do this but cannot explain why. It will just be useful; if and when the time comes that it is needed, it will be ready. The constitution grows steadily word by word, and at last it is put to rest in a big mahogany cabinet.

Meanwhile, Ina Houtzagers has had enough of the restlessness of her husband. She listens as he shares his thoughts and struggles.

"They could do it in Kootwykerbroek. They have started one here in Kootwyk, so why can't they do it in Harskamp?" she reasons.

"You think that's so easy? There is no money, and a school needs capital."

"You don't have to start with a new building. Why not use a house? If you could attract a certified teacher, that would be a place to start."

He laughs. "You women think it is so easy, but there is much more to it than that."

Her thoughts return to her childhood days in Amsterdam where her father, the notary, often said that money spent is money earned. Buying and selling – risking, borrowing, hard work, and perseverance – that is the nature of business.

Dominee Jan Houtzagers has no money to spare or to risk. While his father was alive his family lived without cares, but after his death money was scarce, particularly when the sons were students. His mother spent cautiously and counted every penny, teaching financial restraint to her children.

Ina takes him to task. "Do you believe that God holds the whole world in his hand? Then how can you doubt that he controls the work of his kingdom? If all the money comes from God, and if you begin without any but plan well and work responsibly, why is your only concern about the cost?"

"Maybe you are right," he says thoughtfully, "But it also says in the Bible that no one begins to build a tower without counting the cost."

"You could also figure this way," she counters. "You know the people are willing to pay for the yearly union collection, you know that parents want to live up to their baptismal promise – do you need more security that that? Just begin and let God do the rest. We can trust His promises. Has He failed us yet?"

She sits quietly, deep in thought. "Sometimes I think God stirs us up so we will not become complacent, but learn to plead and struggle and contend with Him. I believe the time has come when people will move on from their rigid ideas. I am convinced we are living in a time of change and progress." Ina's urban background has given her ideas that differ from the common mindset of the Veluwe, but her views sometimes bring clarity to the issues.

Early in the year 1893, at a meeting of the Kootwyk school board, Chairman Houtzagers presents a plan to organize a school in Harskamp. A lengthy discussion follows. Houtzagers will no longer tolerate dithering and delays – a decision must be made, a decision to trust in the Lord. The clouds of pipe smoke rise to the ceiling, a sure sign of deep thought and serious talk. Finally they come to an agreement. Through faith, as the Bible says, we can move mountains. With the help of God, they will face the mountain of troubles to come and they will start a school in Harskamp. They decide to advertise and recruit members for a society for Christian education in Harskamp. In a few days, Ds. Houtzagers will conduct the Sunday service in Trui's house.

When Sunday arrives, a hum of voices greets the dominee as he approaches and finds the small room crammed with people. Trui has coffee ready, and the heater warms the room. Houtzagers sees neither coffee not heater, but walks straight to Trui. "We have plans, solid plans, and will announce it in the service. The Kootwyk school board is planning to start a school here in Harskamp!"

Trui is speechless – a rare occurrence. She thinks of all the years of teaching, all her problems and worries about the inspector, her concerns about how the school would continue if she had to quit, the final acceptance that it was not up to her if it failed....

"Trui, say something.... I think you've had a shock."

"Dominee, this is too much. I see now that I had to wait until the Lord's time for all to come out well."

After the sermon, the announcement is made to the congregation and the invitation is extended to become members of the school society. Trui sees the gladness and enthusiasm. A school, she thinks, a Christian school – I have nothing more, nothing else to ask for....

CHAPTER EIGHTEEN

Fulfillment

The project is not without risk. It is said the Lord will do it if we just ask, but one still must calculate the costs before beginning construction. The Bible says to pray and work. Meetings, advertising, and consultation with the Ede school board all lead to one conclusion: the greatest concern is the need to raise money. The Harskamp people are not enthusiastic. They say, "We still have old Trui, who is doing a fine job. If we build a new school and we hire a new teacher who turns out to be incompetent, what have we gained?"

Trui takes it upon herself to visit the naysayers. She assures them, "I have enough wits about me to decide very quickly if a teacher is not worth his salt. He will not last long, I promise you that."

Trui is not as confident deep down as she would have them believe, but Ds. Houtzagers gives her abundant support. Whenever he comes to Harskamp for a Sunday service, he spends time in lengthy discussions over coffee with her. Ds. Wagenaar also visits with Trui when he is in the area. She arranges for him to conduct some lectures on Christian education.

The people of Harskamp learn about the thoughts and ideas spreading across the country and about the Christian school movement in particular. How difficult, and yet how amazing it is that nickels and dimes, quarters and pennies pour in to make it happen! The buildings are inadequate and the teachers poorly paid, but the classrooms are filled and the curriculum is based on a solid foundation.

Young dominee Vonkenberg, who later becomes a leader of the church's youth organization, travels on foot one certain Sunday to preach at Harskamp. Filled with youthful enthusiasm, he is keen to work for the church and its young people. He promises to come and preach on more occasions, even though the worshippers sit on makeshift benches beneath smoked pork sides and sausages suspended from the rafters. On weekdays he comes to spend time with the children and youth, for he feels the years between ten and twenty are decisive in a person's later life. Their formal education ends at the sixth grade, leaving a crucial gap before adulthood. At this time the seed is sown in his mind that will grow and flower into the Reformed Youth Organization.

"The people of Harskamp are supportive of our plans," Trui says to the newly formed committee, "But they are anxious about undertaking a major project. I think we need a committee member who can manage construction. The person who comes to mind is mijnheer Knuttel."

Knuttel is a well-to-do landowner, familiar in the Harskamp district. They visit him to explain their plans, and he assures them of his cooperation. This positive beginning leads to further planning, and like a boat passing through a lock, one thing leads to the next and they are underway.

It is just before Christmas 1893 when the headmaster of the Kootwyk school presides at an organizational meeting. Prior to the meeting, at his home, Jan Hendrik Bouw opens the heavy door of the family cabinet and withdraws the handwritten pages on which he has spent many long evenings. At the meeting, the committee presents a summary of all the preparatory work. The opinions of the people of the district from near and far have been heard, and the consensus is, "Proceed carefully; we are in favour of the plan, for we see that the need is great."

In that moment, Trui realizes that a new chapter in her life has begun. Her whole life up to now has been directed toward her school; however, it was not done for her own prestige, but always and only for the sake of the children's education.

"Let your spirit be my constant guide," (Psalm 119). The theme of the evening is sung to guide their plans and decisions; God's commands override all legal and financial concerns. The gavel falls; the decision is made. The room is quiet for this historical moment. Trui sits quietly at the back of the room where the women belong, praying, "Lord, give us your blessing."

The Flowering Almond Rod

The chairman announces, "We will need to draft a constitution for our new society. We should now—" He stops as Jan Hendrik Bouw reaches into the inner pocket of his coat and brings out a handful of papers.

"Chairman, I have been preparing for this moment for some time. A year ago I began to write out my ideas on the aims and principles in an orderly fashion."

The chairman is pleasantly surprised. "Who would have thought of that?! I will read it aloud for this meeting." With only a few alterations, the constitution is approved and signed that same evening. Jan Bouw's hands shake as he dips his pen into the inkwell. He thinks about the many evenings they have met for this seemingly hopeless work in faith. God is good. With joy in his, heart he signs his name.

With all haste, the document will go to Her Majesty Queen Wilhelmina for final authorization. Knuttel is acquainted with the formalities required.

The school board members selected are: Jan Hendrik Bouw – president, Harmen Bruil – secretary, Teunis Onderstal – treasurer, Meeuwis Bouw and Gerrit Hogerwy – board members. De heer Knuttel is chosen to supervise the project, since he has experience in business and the law, and he is influential in the outside world as well as having the confidence of the community.

There is no thought of including Trui. Women are never considered for such positions, and besides that, building a school is men's work. However, it becomes a busy time for Trui. Pol often finds that he has to make his own coffee.

"You oughtn't neglect your own house," he complains. "You're always going somewhere and leaving me sitting here alone."

"It would do you good to get up and out of that chair," answers Trui. "You're getting old and stiff from just sitting there. It would do you good to help out with the school."

He keeps a bitter silence and shakes his head, feeling sorry for himself. Can't Trui see how old he is becoming? Work? Running around for that new school? Did he sell his horse and wagon to a young man just to start on a new job? He sighs deeply. No one understands him. How can Trui even suggest that he work on the new school? With his old back, how could he possibly carry benches and desks? They might expect him to run errands for the school – a letter here, a letter there. How could his old legs manage the strength? Going to meetings? He won't even think about it. Let him stay peacefully next to the stove or on the bench outside to smoke his pipe.

He hears Trui talk about their plans. They have found an empty house that can be remodelled into a school, but when he learns that the house is old, he begins to feel his back pain flaring up. He can just hear her telling him, "You can do the painting." She'd better do it herself – she is strong and ambitious, she doesn't show her sixty-seven years. She looks younger than ever, even though her hair is gray and she has a few wrinkles. Her eyes sparkle, her

The Flowering Almond Rod

calm face is attractive, she has an even temper and a quiet manner. It seems that her faith makes her spirit strong.

As evening falls, Pol glimpses someone outside the window. "Trui, you have a visitor. It looks like Harmen Bruil, so it must be about the school, and I had better go sit somewhere else."

"Don't be ridiculous," says Trui. "You needn't go to the kitchen. Stay in your usual place." With a sense of mischief, she assures him, "They won't put you in the school board. You're too old for that."

He sighs with relief. He is quite uncomfortable around all those school supporters. He fears they may find a job for him, because everyone in Harskamp has work fever, everyone is involved: the blacksmith, the carpenter, the painter, the glazier, the children... all volunteering to convert the old house into a suitable school.

Harmen Bruil takes off his white klompen at the door and enters in his black woollen stocking feet. "Good evening."

"And a good evening to you, Harmen," Trui replies, checking the coffeepot. It still bubbles, so she'll soon serve a cupful.

"How is old Pol these days?" asks Harmen, seating himself on the creaky can chair, stowing his flat black cap beneath it.

Pol turns a gloomy look his way. "What can I say? If you had heard me coughing through the night, you would know my days grow short, my life may suddenly be cut off."

"Come on, now, Pol," Trui interrupts. "You are okay; you eat your meals and drink coffee all day, so you're not dying yet. Don't talk like that – you should face God honestly. While you are still healthy, it is better to rejoice in the Lord than to whine about imaginary illnesses."

"How are you managing?" Harmen addresses Trui.

"Oh, the goats don't produce much milk right now, but that is seasonal. I get by because I'm used to being careful with my money. Let's talk about the school, because that is why you are here, I think."

Harmen lights a cigar. "Of course, what else is there to talk about in Harskamp? The school keeps everyone busy and happy."

"When will it open?"

"Possibly on June 1, but there is much work yet to be done. We discovered a leak in the roof, but it has been fixed. We cut an opening into the annex because it's a bearing wall, and that might make the whole building collapse."

"Well, leave it then. We can use it for book storage and the children's coat room."

"Good," Harmen agrees. "Now, Trui, I'm here on business. We decided at the board meeting to place an advertisement in the paper for a headmaster, a certified person. At first we talked about an assistant as well, but that would cost too much. So it was decided to hire a headmaster to do everything for a yearly salary of five hundred guilders."

"That should be plenty," Trui observes. "What a lot of money! Can we raise that much?"

The Flowering Almond Rod

Harmen reckons that a family can barely manage on that amount. They would like to pay more, but it is not possible. "You mustn't think about your younger days when money was worth much more; everything is so expensive nowadays...."

Trui thinks it over. Harmen is probably right, but thrift is not a bad thing.

"The board has also decided to hire a woman to teach handcrafts – mending, knitting, and so on for fifty guilders per year."

Trui thinks about it. That amount sounds more reasonable, and the girls have to learn knitting. She has taught countless children to knit – more than one generation of women and their daughters have come to show her sweaters and stockings.

"If you receive replies soon," she says hopefully, "Then school can begin on June 1st."

"Oh," Harmen says with a smile, "We have one already. We decided to ask you to teach the handcrafts."

Trui is surprised. "But I'm not certified."

"We felt it wasn't necessary. The way we see it, the girls need good knitting skills for their role in household management. When I see the excellent items my wife has made – I appreciate her work so much—"

"Listen," Trui responds decisively, "I have always told the children in school that knitting and scrubbing floors are necessary, but there is more to life. A person must not limit herself to the washboard and broom. No, a person must read – read the Bible, newspapers, books.... If we have a teacher who doesn't understand this, I will continue as before."

"Calm down, Trui," cautions Harmen. "Who says we will appoint an incompetent teacher? We will let you talk to him before we give him the job, I promise. But what about yourself? Will you accept the job? Three times a week from twelve to one you can teach the girls while the boys are dismissed."

Happiness floods Trui's countenance. "Gladly. I'll be happy to do that. I would miss the children if there was nothing for me to do." She pauses to think. "But you do not have to pay me. Keep the money for—"

The armchair creaks – Pol has been listening. "Just like I thought, Trui. It figures. You don't appreciate money. I'm convinced you make a mistake by refusing your pay. So often you asked the Lord for help when you had no money, but now you throw away a chance to earn it. You are a clever woman, so use your head."

"Pol, you should be in the government the way you can talk. I am impressed," Harmen Bruil laughs. "Yes, Trui, your husband is right. The Bible says that the labourer is worthy of his hire."

Trui gives in. Now that they use her own weapon, the Bible, she is defeated. She knows the money will be welcome, so much for the foster children, so much for the sick, and some for the children who have no wool for knitting. They will gladly learn to knit if someone supplies needles, black

The Flowering Almond Rod

wool for stockings, and mending yarn. Always poor, always enough – such is life for Trui.

What seemed impossible for a long time has now become a rallying call for Harskamp. The community prepares for the opening of the school.

When de heer Horstman reads of the event in his Courant, the astonishment is written on his face. He reads the article again. This cannot be possible – how do they dare? A diligent journalist describes the appointment of a school board and the renovation by volunteers of an old house. Of course, preachers are the driving force. Without a dominee, they wouldn't know how to go about the process, and naturally there is a dominee on the school board. He thinks of the saying, "No ministers on the school board, no teachers in the church council – then there will be peace." Oh yes, these people are well organized: they have appointed an official collector of funds, who will travel about the country. A well-dressed beggar for the school – what a job!

Then there's an advertisement for a headmaster, not just an assistant, so all the work will be done alone. Ah, I see someone has accepted. Let's see: G. Kamerling has been appointed and will begin May 1, 1894, and will reside in Harskamp. That young man will soon apply for another position when he sees what the job entails.

Next there's an ad for parents to enrol their children to the Harskamp Christian School. A roster of activities has been planned, yes, yes. Horstman's blood pressure shoots up when he reads the plans: June 1st opening of the school – the school? What a joke! What will it be? An old abandoned hut? He reads on.... They invite all interested persons to attend the opening – oh yes. Who will be curious enough? Educators, school board members – Christian or secular. Who knows? They may even be so foolish as to invite him. He will certainly not attend. Annoyed, he folds the paper. Those disrupters of public education, those psalm-singing fanatics, will never get their act together, but they don't give up, even laden down with expenses.

That Trui – will the poor soul still have a place there? Quickly he opens the paper: oh no! As handcraft instructor, they have named Geertruida van de Pol – Straatman, ordinarily know as Trui.

Mevrouw Horstman enters the room, followed by the maid pushing a laden teacart.

"Thank you, Aggie, I will pour the tea," she says, dismissing the maid. Obviously something is irritating her husband.

"Here, read this." Horstman indicates the notice in the paper. "Read it, or rather, I will read it to you to give you the full import. Remember we talked about the times and circumstances we live in? Obedience and proper order disappear with the ruthless uprising of the lower classes. The government has ruled against Christian schools, the court has imposed fines, and still that school in Harskamp persists."

As he reads out the notice, he notices a line: "There will be treats for the children to make the occasion festive.... Hmpf. Those will surely be Christian treats."

Mevrouw looks outside. She doesn't quite understand her husband's fury. Times are changing, that is clear... she just hopes never to have to look for another housemaid. But to start a self-supporting school?

"What could be wrong with that?" she asks quietly. "It only means less expense for other communities. Let them muddle along. And I think it's nice of them to give the children candy." She twists her rings around her fingers. "I could help handing out the treats. It wouldn't cost us any—"

"Vrouw!" he threatens, slamming the paper down. "I'm sorry I shared my problems with you. I thought you might understand, but women typically react without thinking. I will have more tea, please."

She busies herself with the tea service, graciously pouring the tea into the fine china cups. Was that such a ridiculous suggestion? Wouldn't it be better to help each other, especially those poor people? Why all this fighting? Why is the one party always right and the other one wrong? Why can't we reach out in tolerance and help each other build society? Is the idea so foolish that it is not worth discussing with her husband? She smiles, knowing her husband has confidence in his political party, the government, the school authorities, and the county council of Ede.

Horstman was often impatient with the foot-dragging of the officials. He should have stopped Trui long ago or had her locked up for her stubbornness. Decisions were never implemented; obviously the woman intimidated them.

Mevrouw Horstman's social circle includes wives of the councillors. In the drawing rooms, secrets are shared with whispers and giggles, so she knows that some councillors purposely put the issue under the rug, appearing to agree with the decisions. She knows why no more fines were levied – Trui has a legal right to continue with her Rooster book and her harmonium. She will never reveal her suspicion that her husband dreads another confrontation with Trui.

Mevrouw thinks about the old woman, Trui of Harskamp, who simply maintained her school for twenty-four years and never gave up, who never let anyone intimidate her into stopping. She persisted toward her goal in her own stubborn way. The new school board, the minister – none could equal the heroism of this humble farm wife, who laid the foundation for the school in Harskamp.

CHAPTER NINETEEN

Struggles

June 1st, 1984. Thirty-three pupils are enrolled. Harskamp celebrates. Invited guests include public officials who have come from as far as Ede. Carriages and covered wagons crowd the roadside, while horses are tied to fence posts. Children play in the sunshine and under the freshly leafed-out trees. A haze hangs over the fields, yellow with buttercups as they stretch out to the horizon. White-blossomed shrubs promise mid-summer blackberries.

Trui wears her Sunday best black apron; her bonnet is spotlessly white and stiff with starch, pleated perfectly and tied under her chin. Pol wears his black suit and flat cap.

"A person should look their best for a celebration," Trui comments.

Pol chuckles, "Just look at us! I feel like a gentleman."

"I didn't mean that, just that we should look our best. The Bible even says to wear special garments for celebration."

He nods agreeably – the easiest way to get along. He married a wife who knows the Bible from memory.

Ge Verhoog

He shuffles toward the barnyard. The goat is grazing, the chickens cluck happily, and the weather is fine. Trui takes a last look at her old school room at the back of the barn. For twenty-four years she has taught reading, writing, and Bible verses here. Her pupils learned to recite the Ten Commandments fluently, and they memorized prayers for mealtime and bedtime, all so that they would know God as their father in Heaven, who watches over small and great and helps them through life. They don't need this room for school anymore, only for church services. The lectern can stay for now. Her school is over.

"But now, Lord," she prays, "You have made all things so wonderful, how can we thank you enough for the beginning of a new school, where children will learn all they need to know? My school is gone, because you must become more and I must become less – as it should be. My heart overflows." She closes the door.

In the afternoon, viewing the new school with Pol, she is amazed at how the old house has been improved.

"Your school was all right," Jan assures Trui. "It just became too small, but now your cares are over, I must say."

Trui is silent. Very few people can guess another's thoughts. But why should one always reveal what is on her mind? Often it isn't even important.

The evening hours are spent listening to speakers and socializing. Meester Kamerling, headmaster and assistant in one, appears calm and friendly. Trui examines his words and manner carefully and decides he may be all right. But she will wait and see, not judge hastily.

He addresses her as Juffrouw van de Pol. Trui corrects him, feeling the title to be too grand. "Listen, this is just a small village and I am used to the ordinary title of Vrouw. Better still, just call me Trui, like everyone else."

Dominee Houtzagers is not present at this joyful occasion. He is in poor health and his body cannot keep up with the events his spirit has inspired. The Knuttels, husband and wife, receive public appreciation. Chaired by de heer van Velzen, instructor of religion in Ede, the gathering overflows with thanksgiving. Van Velzen expounds on the reasons why Christian schools are essential in the land.

De heer Kamerling proves to be an organized and interesting speaker in the second speech of the evening. The listeners pay careful attention to his words. Trui, who with Pol has found a seat near the back, nods in agreement – he will be a good teacher. She also notes that he could lead well in a church service. This man speaks without hesitation and he seems to be humble, not one who loves to hear himself talk – Trui cannot abide that.

Now and then Trui lets her eyes wander around the schoolroom, where the children soon will sit in their desks, receiving a bona fide education. She sighs with relief, thinking the shadow of the school inspector is gone.

The closet has been converted to a storage room to hold the slates and chalk, the readers and the Bibles. Trui is happy about the Bibles – without them, Kamerling told her, he would not be a teacher here.

Her old Rooster book has been put away as a keepsake or to be used with her grandchildren. They get into mischief if there is nothing to do, so the book will be handy. Mina's little Jan and Hendrik – are they not clever? They listen with happy faces when she tells them stories, and they love to come to her house.

It is time for a break, a brief pause to relax. Chairs scrape, pipes are lit, and Trui hands out sweets to keep the children awake and out of mischief.

The head of the school in Ede speaks next – he points out the responsibility of the parents for their baptised children. At last the Kootwykerbroek headmaster gives a broad overview of the difference between public and Christian education.

"Are there more to come?" Pol whispers to Trui. "By now I know all I ever want to know about Christian education."

"Quiet," Trui admonishes him. "Be glad this evening has come."

The final speaker concludes with the affirmation that everyone is happy that this day has arrived, the celebration is over, and school can now commence.

"What a wonderful evening," comments one of the departing guests. "I was almost sorry to hear the man say amen; I could have listened much longer."

The Flowering Almond Rod

Elsewhere in Ede, mijnheer Horstman, in good humour, and van Limmen, who happens to be in Ede, meet together as they raise clouds of cigar smoke.

Meanwhile, in the remodelled house-schoolroom, amidst cheaply purchased books and slates, the people stand and joyfully sing a psalm of thanks to God.

As Trui and Pol walk homeward together, Pol remarks, "They had a thank you for every stranger, even the Knuttels, and not a word about you."

Trui shushes him with a hand on his arm. "Still, if the Lord has used me, they needn't thank me, it's all right. After all, I still work at the school and hope to continue for a long time yet... our Harskamp school." She looks up to where the treetops reach to the sky. She will never forget this evening – her hopes are fulfilled.

The next morning, as she watches the children walk to the new school, they wave at her and she waves back with a happy smile. Then it is nine o'clock. Classes have begun and she must do her housework before she goes to teach her handicraft lesson at twelve. Preparing her material – sock wool, needles, unbleached cotton, sewing needles, and thread – she is happy to work with the children of Harskamp.

Trui has fewer responsibilities now, no more need to clean her schoolroom three times a week, and no more concern for the quality of the children's education. Her only work is to prepare the room on Saturday for the church service and clean up on Monday. What a nice life!

She has time to read the whole newspaper, and when Pol feels too old, she reads the news to him. The railway controversy continues to make the headlines. The rivalry between the two companies is settled with the abandonment of the Rijn Railway and the dominance of the Holland Iron Railway Company. "Amsterdam has won," Trui reasons, "And soon the capital will run lines in all directions."

"Nothing but pride," Pol sighs. "People are never satisfied."

Trui regards him over her reading glasses. "You don't know the difference between pride and improvement. The Bible teaches us to build and look to the future – that is not pride, it is progress."

"What good does it do me to see such a devilish thing roaring by? At that speed you won't be able to breathe – you will choke – and can you be responsible for that?"

Trui laughs. "The passengers don't even feel the wind, because the carriages are closed."

Pol's mouth turns down. "Closed wagons? Just think how stuffy that will be – you won't be able to take a breath. I heard of one passenger who could not get on because the train left too early. By his watch, the train should not have left for half an hour." He shakes his head. "That's not right. His watch agreed with the town clock, which is always right – the railway should give in. And then – the conductor said the train was leaving. The passenger said, 'Wait till I finish this beer that I've already paid for. But the train didn't wait.'"

Pol is quiet. If he had money, he wouldn't mind having some beer to drink. But then he would have to explain to Trui, who would only say it's a good thing he has none so he won't fall into temptation.

Trui folds up the paper and looks over her glasses at the clock. "Bedtime." She closes the shutters, locks the door, and takes up her Meditations. Pol hurries off to bed. "Still, it is a wonderful invention," she muses. "To go from Utrecht to Amsterdam by train, later all the way to Arnhem… soon we'll have a station here."

Pol interrupts her fantasies. "I hope my old eyes won't see that. It is just too much for my aching bones. Harskamp is already so busy, why is a horse-drawn wagon not enough? People should be satisfied with what they have."

Trui suspects that the advent of the railway could be a disadvantage to her. The school inspector needn't travel by horse and buggy through the loose sand now that the train provides comfortable travel to Utrecht, Ede, and Arnhem.

"Have you been to Harskamp lately?" inquires Horstman one morning. He should be able to visit the schools in a day without staying overnight.

"I am on my way today," Limmen informs him. "I have to see what became of that school of Trui's." Horstman is curious as well.

By afternoon of the same day, two fine gentlemen sporting canes and top hats are seen strutting along the winding Harskamp road. They pause before the newly opened Christian school.

Meester Kamerling feels uneasy, and Trui, just finished her handicraft lesson, stands with hands on her hips, regarding them.

"That is the woman Trui," Limmen whispers to his companion, who notices the strained atmosphere.

"Just the type I expected," Horstman replies quietly.

"What does this mean?" Trui asks as the gentlemen approach the door.

"We are here for an inspection," Limmen announces. "I am the school inspector."

"I know that," Trui tells him stiffly.

"Are you the headmaster here?" he asks Kamerling.

He replies with a brief bow. "My name is Kamerling."

Without invitation, they step into the schoolroom. Trui's eyes glitter angrily, but Kamerling calms her. "We must allow this, and why not? Everything is in order."

The visitors inspect the low desks, the storage room, the small window, the sagging wall, and the roof that seems to need support. Harskamp has restored what could be fixed, but the building is showing its age.

"We have seen it. Goodbye." With measured steps, they return to the road where their ride awaits.

"What a pair!" Trui exclaims. "What were they doing here?"

"Central control of the schools," Kamerling guesses. "Why aggravate them? Forget about them. We will continue as usual because we have our school, and that's enough."

A few days later a letter for the headmaster arrives from the inspector. Trui reacts with fear when Kamerling comes to her door that evening with the letter. "You don't come with good news." She tries to hide her worry. "Come in."

Kamerling looks pale. He unfolds the letter and reads: "The inspector has visited the separate school in Harskamp and has found that education has improved by having a certified teacher, that there is adequate equipment, and the children are learning to read. However, it is his responsibility to state that the building does not pass inspection, being in a state of collapse, thus endangering the children within; therefore, he deems it necessary to rule that the school be closed and that the parents are to provide a suitable classroom which adheres to approved safety standards. This must be done immediately, because the school cannot operate in its present condition."

Deep stillness accompanies the careful folding of the letter Kamerling has finished reading. The school, just started with such enthusiasm. Another building – who will supply the money? It took so much effort to get this house ready.

"The school has been in operation for twenty-seven days," Kamerling groans. "Our opponents just don't give up."

Trui moves her chair toward the table, twisting her handkerchief nervously. "Well, that's that. I always say that even the greatest city began with shanties. We have to go and look for a more suitable building."

"But the money?" Kamerling asks. "The moving, remodelling, and furnishings?"

"I don't know that either. I only know that we will continue on." She looks at him directly. "Did you think we could manage the school without trouble? Don't you believe it. I only know that we have more help than all the school inspectors combined. Let's talk to the board chairman first."

"Why don't you sleep on it a night?" Pol suggests, pulling nervously on his empty pipe. "Be careful, Trui, that they don't put you in jail."

Trui nods in agreement. "You make a wise suggestion."

Rather than sleep, the night is one of searching for solutions. Trui will never give up, but the Lord is trying them severely to see if they can withstand the storm of opposition. They decide to take the letter to the board.

Next day, the board meets at the home of Harmen Bruil to discuss ways and means and consider influential citizens who could be of assistance. Baron van Pallandt does not socialize with the common folk of Harskamp, but may be interested in helping. Mijnheer Knuttel will approach him concerning an unused carriage house on his estate. Knuttel finds out that he is willing to rent it for one hundred guilders per year. The remodelling will be the board's responsibility.

Teunis Onderstal, the treasurer who has spent many an evening totting up the pennies and nickels, objects. "That's impossible. We cannot raise that much money."

Harmen Bruil glares at him but holds his temper. They have only a short while before the inspector makes his next visit. He will be asking Harmen Bruil when a new building will be in use. When he asks, "Do you have another building?" Harmen's response will be "Of course we do!"

The inspector will have to be satisfied with that. He will never know that any difficulties and quarrels have occurred in Harskamp.

Knuttel calls the board, including Trui, together. "As a board we just cannot raise the money," he begins. "There are no more funds, but I have a suggestion: I can privately rent the building and let the school use it. There is, however, one condition – it may not be used as a church."

"That's all right," Trui states, "We can just continue to use my home. The benches and the lectern are still there. The Sunday school just begun by Meester Kamerling can be held in the new building as long as it presents no problems." The young teacher blushes. "I promise to take responsibility. I believe the dominee from Otterloo will teach catechism after school hours in the building."

"It seems everything is organized. Is there anything else?" asks Trui.

A huge feeling of relief settles over the gathering. They wonder why they were so worried.

"Sometimes the answer is ready before we even ask," Harmen Bruil remarks. "We can always trust the future rests in God's hand."

"And we can leave it in God's hand," Trui adds.

Harmen Bruil does the necessary carpentry, and volunteers set to work to prepare the new building – another active and joyful time.

On an icy cold day in January, the inspector makes another trip to Harskamp. He makes his way over crunching snowdrifts, facing a bone-chilling east wind toward the carriage house that is now the school.

Trui drops a few stitches of the black stocking she is knitting, then pushes her glasses back into place. "Children, just keep on knitting – needle in, thread over, pull it through, and slide it to the other needle."

Meester Kamerling shows the inspector around, saying very little. It seems that Limmen has found nothing to criticize as he prepares to leave. All he says is, "You should keep the rooms warmer, and you should teach the children to stand up and greet me when I enter."

Kamerling replies politely, "I will see to that, sir."

Discussing the event with Trui later, they conclude that the inspector's report was appropriate. "Then we should be all right with minor corrections."

The community continues to struggle with the school's finances. The money collector resigns – there is talk that he has pocketed some of the funds – and a

The Flowering Almond Rod

replacement collector must be found. The widow Elbertje Bouw-Zandbergen, mother of the board members Jan and Meeuwis Bouw, offers an interest-free loan of two hundred guilders. This relieves some of the pressure, but a large part of the debt remains.

"It doesn't matter," Trui insists when she hears the report at the meeting. "I know what it is to be without a cent, but I always managed somehow."

Adult evening classes for ages twelve to thirty keep the benches occupied in the winter and Meester Kamerling busy teaching reading and arithmetic.

De heer Knuttel has been the liaison between the board and Baron van Pallant, but his work necessitates a move away from Harskamp.

Ds. Houtzagers remains in Kootwyk, declining to serve other communities, for he feels he is still needed. He takes over for Knuttel and provides stalwart support for Harskamp.

The practice of certain board members to visit the school every third month has dwindled. As one tells it, "Why should we keep doing this? The children learn to read and write capably even in the upper grades. We have no complaints – we were thrilled to hear them sing the national anthem 'Het Wilhelmus.'"

The number of students is growing, as well as the problems that go with growth, but no one notices. He teaches seventy children in three age groups and has to divide his time between them.

When Kamerling describes his heavy workload at the next meeting, the people are sympathetic. The teacher should know what is best for the children, and if the work is too much for one person, they must find another teacher. They place an advertisement, but it is difficult to attract anyone to such an isolated place. Finally a student volunteer arrives, but as soon as a paying position is offered elsewhere, he is gone. Still, the school pioneers on. Pioneers must plod through the heat of the day, working the raw land and ploughing midst the rocks. Yet there is joy in the unyielding land when one has a view of the broad heavens above.

CHAPTER TWENTY

Trui Steps Down

The population of the country is on the increase. New houses appear in every town and village, the churches experience a spirit of renewal, and even quiet little Harskamp is affected by the migration away from crowded cities toward open areas with wider horizons. The newcomers often have different ideas and lifestyles, leading to misunderstandings and criticism of each other's ways.

The original Harskampers have experienced the years of Trui's struggle for the Christian school. Everyone lent a hand in the culminating effort to get the school on its feet; it has become a symbol of their community spirit. Trui has an acknowledged place as their handcraft instructor – they know and trust her, suspicious of any replacement. Who says what is new is always better? They know what they have. For years Trui has taught the children to knit and sew. Her wrinkled hands have picked up many dropped stitches, and she patiently repeats the steps: needle in, yarn over, pull it through, slip to the other needle. Knitting is not as easy as it looks.

Harmen Bruil dreads the visit he must make as chairman of the board. At the board meeting yesterday, Trui was absent. Arthritic pain, worse than usual, kept her home from the meeting, a rare occurrence. She now sits at the table when Harmen arrives.

"Good day, Trui."

"And the same to you. What's the matter? Another visit from the inspector?"

Harmen laughs. "That's your evil spirit, I think. He did his worst to make it so, but no, we have not seen or heard from him since his last visit."

"He'd be wiser to stay away," Trui grumbles.

"Now we have another problem," Harmen begins carefully. "Life is made up of changes, and at every turn there is another battle." He observes her thoughtfully. She has had a difficult life, but has never given up. Her straight form has stooped slightly, but her spirit is alert. The errand that brings him here weighs greatly on him.

"Now then," he sighs heavily, "The annual meeting was well attended, and the parents are satisfied with the progress the children are making in reading, writing, arithmetic, and so on."

Trui nods. "Yes, I couldn't teach the number work because I didn't know it well enough myself. I'm happy the teacher does that now, otherwise they'd have to go to Otterloo."

The Flowering Almond Rod

"Some of the newcomers, you know, in the new houses, those that moved here from the city, they've been talking, well, the teaching is okay, but...."

Trui looks narrowly at him from over her spectacles, and her hand clenches inside the sock she's mending. "Just say what's bothering you, Harmen."

"Anyway, they were talking about you – they want the children to learn different handcrafts."

Her fist in the sock thumps the table. "What now?" She is upset. "Is there no end to the complaints? Are they still not happy?"

"Ah, Trui, you know how it is, just let them chatter."

"But you still had to come and tell me about it."

"I had to promise; they insisted, you see."

It is quiet in the room. She pokes the needle into her mending, but her aim is erratic. "What am I doing that's wrong?" she asks finally, with a strained note in her voice.

"Doing wrong?" says Harmen. "Trui, please understand we find no fault, but the newcomers have city ideas – they don't wear home-knitted socks, they want lace trimming and so on, and they want to learn that."

Trui nods. "I think that's it." She speaks thoughtfully. "I think the newcomers want everything real – a real teacher, which we have already; a real dominee, who is often here on Sunday; and now they want a real teacher with a diploma, not an old farmwife like me." She looks at him sharply. "Harmen, the situation is, the people are becoming proud and arrogant."

Harmen says nothing; the objections are very serious. They think Trui is inadequate. She has heard this all her life – not capable, not certified – yet she has done more than all the critics together.

"Tell me everything," she insists.

"What can I say? During the question period, a new couple stood and said they would like to enrol their children, but that you were too old and incapable." He stops, shocked by his own words.

Trui feels he does not want to tell her, but she wants to know. "Did everyone agree with them?"

"Not at all," Harmen hastens to assure her. "The entire board and many others called in chorus, 'Trui must stay, we can't lose her.'. Then I asked that all in favour of keeping you on please stand, and nearly everyone stood up."

"How many remained sitting?" Oh, she wished that her arthritis hadn't kept her from attending.

"Not many."

She thought about that. "Not many, but it is the beginning. Yes, times are changing, and our quiet little town of Harskamp will never be the same again. We are being carried along into modern life – just read the newspapers. We cannot escape it. The tail of every hurricane swings dangerously about."

Harmen blows a cloud of pipe smoke toward the bacon sides hanging from the ceiling. Trui suspects he has more on his mind. "The entire gathering supported you, Trui, but those newcomers spoke so convincingly, we decided to try

The Flowering Almond Rod

something new. If it doesn't work, you will regain your position, but anyway, they would like the teacher's wife to work together with you."

"Juffrouw Kamerling?" Her eyes open wide in amazement.

He nods. "Do you have a problem with her?"

"No," she whispers, "No." She sighs deeply and her hands shake. I must be sensible, she reminds herself.

Harmen stands. "I've said what I must, but be assured we all stand behind you."

Trui nods, somewhat overcome. "Yes, Harmen, you say you stand behind me, but I always have to go first."

After he leaves, Trui sits alone in the room, hands motionless in her lap. Incompetent. Incapable. The words cut like sharp knives in her soul – the pain wounds deeply. Twenty-four years they let her work with hardly any encouragement. For twenty-four years she taught countless children to read, to depend on the Bible, to write so they could send letters to their own children later. So many mothers did all their own knitting because she had patiently guided their little hands. It is so difficult to think she may have to leave the school. Her task is done; she is no longer needed. She sees the room through a gray mist, and a tear rolls down her wrinkled cheek, a hard-won tear.

"O Lord," her heart cries, "Help me, I have been through so much, but this is too much." Then she feels a deep rage against people who judge so mercilessly, who know nothing of the community of Harskamp. They think only of paper certificates and have no understanding of people. What is wisdom? What is knowledge?

If any of you desires wisdom, let him ask of God, the Bible says. Understanding suddenly dawns, her fist relaxes.... She fumbles for her handkerchief. The Lord knows all things; He sees all things; He knows she did not work for herself. She was so eager to serve, so zealous, but it was for nothing. For nothing? Not at all. The school still stands, not always steadily, but the work goes on. There are daily struggles – every day has enough. So many children, so few teachers, assistants leave too soon, money is scarce, yet they continue on faithfully because they work for God's cause.

Why am I so upset? Trui asks herself. Why do critical words cause so much pain? Is it just because things don't go my way? All the years of effort, they were not for her but for the school. But what will happen if the people of Harskamp begin to doubt the value of the school? Lord, I am so confused, so worried, yet I must believe you are in control. I must leave it up to you. If a new teacher is chosen, may she do her work well so that I can retire with an easy mind. I pray that she will not work for status, position, or money, but to serve you and the children. Your glory must grow as I decline. I pray that you will always remember your children.

CHAPTER TWENTY-ONE

Growth

Remarkably, the government has decided to subsidize the Christian schools, but because of mismanagement, the application was sent in too late. "I even traveled to den Haag myself," reports a board member. "I spoke with the officials, but they all tell me it is too late. So I told them to keep their money – it is hardly worth the bother."

"You talk foolishness," Trui says to the group of men standing around. Her class is about to begin, but this matter must be discussed. "I don't understand you men," she scolds. "How can you be so careless when every cent counts? When you can finally receive help from the government, you think it hardly worthwhile!"

All in all, they are deep in debt again. "Trui is right," says Meeuwis Bouw, "When you add up all that is needed for the winter, as well as firewood and coal for the teacher's house."

"When will the heater be cleaned out?" inquires Kamerling, "And the leaky roof repaired?"

Teunis Onderstel makes notes. "I will inform Harmen about the heater and the roof. Van Driesten, the smith, can fix them. Jan Bouw can see to the firewood, and I will bring coal or have someone bring it. What else? Oh yes, kerosene." He pushes his spectacles to his forehead. After much discussion, they decide to buy kerosene from van Galen.

Trui is amazed when Kamerling announces, "The ten guilders for my wife for helping Trui – you can cancel that."

"Why?" asks Harmen Bruil. "Should I change the budget?"

"Yes, change it," the teacher replies cheerfully, "Because my wife is quitting since Trui does an excellent job alone."

"You see, Trui," says Harmen, "They cannot do without you."

"I think they can, but it feels good to be appreciated. The school is near to my heart." Strange, she thinks, how we expect a hurricane in a dark cloud and then it turns into a breath of fresh air.

"Next Sunday I will lead the worship service at Trui's home," Kamerling says. "It's another way we can cut costs."

"Be sure to ask him often," comments treasurer Onderstel. "It saves money, and the people love to hear him."

Kamerling has forfeited fifty guilders per year, because he can manage without it, since his wife has the ability to get five cents' worth out of every penny. Not many in his position would do his job for so little, and yet in addition,

The Flowering Almond Rod

he volunteers his time and effort to preach on Sunday to save the minister's fee. It is an awesome responsibility to work in God's vineyard, the most awesome thing about it being that the workers persist in their labours in spite of poor recompense.

Kamerling tells himself that God has given everything freely, so why should he expect payment?

We have a good teacher, Trui thinks. He fits in well with us. He leads a service as skilfully as any minister, he drinks very little of the glass of water Trui supplies every Sunday, and when he doesn't use much, she puts it back in the cupboard for next time. Water doesn't spoil.

"We ought to ask the church in Otterloo to have a collection for our school," suggests Harmen Bruil. "I will go there and ask them." He harnesses his horse to the cart that evening and meets with some members, but encounters opposition.

"We have needs of our own and have no wealthy supporters, so we feel each town must row with its own oars," they reply.

"That is why I am here," Harmen explains. "We thought we would find support for us in Otterloo."

"We have our own church and school to support. A labourer earns a mere five guilders per week. But you can try to hold a collection and see what happens."

The collection is a disappointment. When Trui asks the treasurer about the amount, he replies, "Not much. It did not take long to count it. All together, two guilders and thirty-nine cents."

Trui claps her hands in dismay. "What a shame. Are they not Christians who have been taught to help each other?" There must be a way. All her life she has scraped to save money and has managed somehow.

She has an idea. When Kamerling has finished the service the following Sunday, she goes to the Sunday school class and talks to the children about the meaning of offerings. "There will be a children's offering for the school next Sunday. Use the money in your piggy banks, look for jobs, ask your parents for spare change."

The adults are amused. "That will be some collection! We'll see next week."

All week the children of Harskamp eagerly seek to earn quarters from the farmers and from anyone who can spare some change. They scrub stoops, feed calves, wash milk pails, fetch medicine for the elderly, and generally make a nuisance of themselves to garner whatever they can for the school collection.

On Sunday, little hands deposit five guilders and forty cents in the collection plate. Trui takes it triumphantly to Teunis the treasurer. He laughs, "Trui knows how to get things done!" He enters the amount with scratchy pen strokes into his ledger. "As long as Trui is in Harskamp we will have an example to follow!"

"The Bible tells us to bring everything to the Lord, and now you see how He has helped us," Trui admonishes. Her belief is made even greater when an unexpected gift of one hundred guilders arrives from Nijkerk.

"A hundred guilders?" exclaims Jan Hendrik Bouw, amazed. "Do you hear that, Teunis? Just like that!"

"The Nijkerk church has decided to designate a thousand guilders for needy schools. We heard from Kootwijk of your need, and thus we felt that Harskamp was deserving of a portion thereof."

"Doesn't it amaze you?" Bouw asks Trui when he brings the good news.

"I am very happy, but amazed?" She smiles sweetly. "Not really – the Lord always provides. The only surprise is the means by which the Lord provides, from sources we don't expect."

Everything will be all right, she muses as she peels her potatoes. The Bible tells us that those who trust in the Lord do not build on shifting sand. The school is not a useless undertaking; the people of Harskamp built the school to serve God. The struggle will go on. No one promised it would be easy, but they do not work alone. Trui recalls a missionary book in which she found stories the children loved to hear. It was called De kruisflag in top (Under the Flag With the Cross). The Christian banner displays that Jesus reigns. What more would a Christian need?

Board chairman Jan Hendrik Bouw decides to leave his farm De Lange Wei (The Long Meadow) and its harsh winters to take up farming near Barneveld. De heer Knuttel takes his place. Knuttel, being a man of means as well as being generous, raises his donation, thus inspiring many others to follow suit. Some supporters did without extras, but felt that providing Christian education for their children was worth some impoverishment.

"That Trui is strange," comments a new resident to his wife. "Have you heard her talk? So typical of this region – so depressing and hyper-religious."

The wife has met her and heard others speak about her. "I thought she opposed that heavy-hearted, pessimistic attitude. Some think her too easygoing."

"But she warns people harshly."

The young woman gazes from the window of her new house at the wide-open fields beyond. "The people who have always lived here have a limited knowledge of the world, but I admire her. She takes the Bible seriously, but is not stuck on tradition."

"What do you mean by that?"

"I mean that in the city our churches just focused on rule after rule, and that was all. Trui understands the gospel, knows it by heart, better than any of us."

He shrugs. "I dislike people who see the hand of God in everything. I think it's overly pious, a type of spiritual illness."

"Illness? You may call it that, but a spiritual illness doesn't have such power. She stops for no one. Did you know she stood up to the court justice? That she has found homes for and supervised many foster children? That

The Flowering Almond Rod

she taught school for twenty-four years for children who would have no education without her work? That's not an illness. When you talk to her, you can tell she speaks with a clear mind."

He laughs dismissively. "I'd rather talk to you."

She disregards him. "It's a shame we call people who are ambitious for the Lord fanatics. Better that we should envy them. Trui is a fighter, and yet she is humble before God."

He lights another cigarette. "It seems you have been taking instruction from Trui. Weren't you one of the complainers about her handcraft lessons?"

"I am sorry about that," she confesses sincerely. "I talked like a fool – I have a lot to learn from her. I envy her dedication."

Trui is unaware of all the talk about her personality and how she lives – it doesn't interest her. She is too busy finding solutions for new problems that arise.

By the end of the year, when the books are balanced, a surplus of thirteen guilders and fourteen cents remain after a total expense of twelve hundred guilders.

They did not build on sand, but on God's faithfulness – that was the crucial factor.

CHAPTER TWENTY-TWO

An Army Chaplain

The village of Harskamp is shaken on its foundations by a new rumour making the rounds. It is hard for the villagers to believe that an army camp and training grounds will appear before the turn of the century in the year 1900.

"How can it be?" wonder the newer residents. "We built our houses here for the peace and quiet, and now we will be disturbed by the booming of artillery and rifle fire."

Gies Butselaar, a sheepherder since age seventeen, predicts no good can come of it: "When the soldiers come, the farms will disappear. But that's life."

Some shake their heads, not knowing where it will lead. Others compare it to a dark storm cloud from the north. "Before you realize it, it will be like Sodom and Gomorrah – all of Harskamp is doomed! If you think you can keep the devil away by building a church, he will build a chapel beside it."

Trui raises her eyebrows. "We haven't built a church here yet," she comments. "We still meet in the back of my barn. And why are you fussing so much about a bunch of soldiers? Who knows, they might organize a marching band. What about that? David in the Bible was a musician." "But they will go too far. I've got nothing against them blaring Christian songs, but they might play worldly music that we can't resist."

"The soldiers will of course come into our stores, our houses, our markets, maybe even to church. Soldiers are not spiritual people – they are dangerous."

Krelis has a unique message to share. "Hear now, I have had a special revelation: Keep sin outside of your door, for it will drag you into Hell. I have warned you."

When Krelis makes his proclamations, his neighbours don't take him seriously. His devout wife Hiltje, now lying in the cemetery, was replaced in such haste they shook their heads in scepticism when he claimed the Lord had led a new wife to him within months of Hiltje's passing, and who was he to resist God's will? A second series of children soon followed the first.

Krelis does not approve of soldiers and the sinful lives they lead. On the other hand, he thinks about all the shoes those soldiers will be wearing, and how they will wear them out when they march. They would need to have them repaired by the local shoemaker, none other than Krelis, who has many hungry children to feed.

Trui is patient with Pol's sighs as he worries about the rumours. "I will soon be eighty, and now I will find no rest;

cannons and bombs and guns and ammunition – I'm sure it will finish me off."

Trui smiles a bit. "You won't go before your time," she soothes. "I don't think they will bother us here."

"Why do you think that?"

"Be sensible. The heather stretches far and wide, and we won't hear a bit of it in the village. They have plenty of room and it's not wartime – it's just training."

Other opinions are being aired in the village. "People should not plan for war. Then the soldiers could live as honest citizens and the heather would remain quiet, unpolluted by gunpowder and undisturbed by noise and traffic," pronounces Bouwman as the men gather under the linden trees in the village square. He has more sympathetic listeners here than at home. His wife has little respect for his wisdom.

Leemhuis is irritated and argues, "Let them play at war – it doesn't bother us. There's enough space on the heather."

"You don't know the deep concerns I have about war," Bouwman insists. "You don't understand! Why do we allow war to happen? It would be better if we went to church and listened to those dominees who speak with wisdom and tell the truth."

Trui has been listening to the discussion. She sets her basket on the ground and places her hand on her hips. "There are reasons to train soldiers," she declares sharply. "War is inevitable; just listen to yourselves."

"What are you talking about?" Bouwman growls.

Not at all intimidated, she replies, "I mean, if you put three Hollanders in a row, within five minutes they will find something to argue about and will be tearing at each other's hair in a fight. That's how you ordinary people here behave, so how can you expect our leaders in power to be different?" She picks up her basket and strides briskly home.

Krelis watches her darkly. "That Trui is a dangerous woman. She does not know her place, and talks about things women know nothing about."

"Trui should have been a man," Bouwman remarks.

Leenhuis laughs boisterously. "It's too bad men aren't more like Trui! She certainly has it all together. If we followed her example, there wouldn't be any need for war, that's my opinion."

In spite of all the warnings and objections, in 1899 the firing range is set up near Harskamp. Soon there are soldiers everywhere. At first people are curious enough to walk over to the range to investigate, but they avoid personal contact with the soldiers. Bored young men wander aimlessly over the heather toward the village when off-duty. The villagers try to ignore them, because soldiers have a reputation for drinking, swearing, and rough behaviour.

Dominee Houtzagers sees that something is not right. A few uniformed soldiers attend the church services at Trui's place, but no one speaks to them. It is not right that a congregation that has received so much help in their need should now turn a cold shoulder to the young men in uniform. They have been conscripted and are being prepared to defend the country in case of war, possibly at the cost of life or limbs, and yet these self-righteous Veluwers have no place in their hearts or homes for them. The dominee despairs of changing their minds, of persuading them to see that a soldier is just someone's son in the army. He discusses it with Kamerling, who agrees that attitudes are difficult to change.

"We have to think of something else," says Kamerling. He has a great idea he hardly dares to utter, but is convinced that dreams may succeed, even though they don't seem sensible at first. "What about a servicemen's center? A military canteen?"

Houtzagers chuckles. "I suppose you want to build a church next."

Kamerling thinks about that. "Harskamp is changing – this military influx is part of the change, and it may be a good thing for the community." Houtzagers agrees. "The school is growing, evening classes and catechism are well attended, and Trui sometimes hosts three services on a Sunday. Soon we must make some serious plans."

"Soon?" asks Kamerling. "Now! There's a building across from Trui's place that would be a good drop-in center. We could build a little chapel beside it for the military. It might be the beginning of a church in Harskamp."

Houtzagers is excited about the ideas. "I'm going to discuss it with Ds. Vonkenberg over in Voorthuizen. That's not far from here, and he's a man who likes to work with young people. We must make plans."

Kamerling, Houtzagers, and Vonkenberg spend many hours in Trui's sitting room discussing ways and means. Trui, without official status, is still able to provide substantial input, and the thick walls of her house keep their plans from spreading.

They decide to combine the servicemen's center with a chapel, under the supervision and with the support of the church of Ede. The Ede church agrees to do this. Next they must select a supervisor for the center who will also serve as a pastor for the chapel, relieving nearby dominees of some responsibility. However, a military chaplain without seminary training will be hard to find. Funding the project is the next hurdle, but they are used to beating rocks to bring forth gold. They seek help from church councils. Ds. Vonkenberg, founder and head of the National Reformed Young Men's Societies, solicits donations from its members. An anonymous interest-free loan of five thousand guilders appears. It is enough to begin the work.

Trui is happy. For the second time her home will be replaced with better facilities. She counts her blessings: a school, a church, a center for the military, and an oefenaar to lead the work.

"Oefenaar?" asks Pol. "What kind of man is that?"

"Neither fish nor fowl." Trui explains, "He is somewhere between a dominee and a layman. He is not an ordained clergyman, but has done some Bible study and has permission to preach and is called an oefenaar."

Pol is not impressed with the idea. "I pity the man, doing the work of a minister for less money."

Trui regards him over her spectacles. "You are such a nitpicker. Working in the service of God may not be as lucrative as other work, but still provides richer rewards than any large bank account."

Pol takes a pull on his empty pipe. "I haven't seen your rich rewards."

"What?" Trui sees red. "That's sinful talk. The sausages and slabs of bacon hang from our rafters, our goat gives plenty of milk, and the chickens keep laying eggs. You smoke your pipe all day and the stove keeps you warm. What more do you want?"

He shrinks under her reprimand. "Now, now, calm down."

"No, I won't calm down. How dare you complain! I have nothing to complain about and I will not – listen to me now – I will not hear a word about going hungry. We've had enough to eat every day, and I believe the Bible promise that 'Those who fear God shall never know want.'" Her face glows with zeal as she defends what God has done for her. There is a lot she can tolerate, but not this.

Pol changes the subject. "How do you find a man for that oefenaar shepherd job, or whatever you call it?"

Trui settles down. Pol is good company but not always easy to talk with. The man is old, and they ought to enjoy their time together. She softens her attitude. "You are right, Pol, a shepherd. The Bible calls God's children His sheep, and Jesus is the good shepherd who guides His sheep. Now He will certainly provide for us a chaplain who will do the shepherd's work."

The room grows quiet. Pol can never understand Trui's plans, but they always work out. This time, though, she is trying too much.

However, there is more hanging over their heads than bacon and sausages. With his eyes half-closed, he says, "Last time Mina was here, she mentioned some news she'd read in the paper."

"What news?"

"The government wants to make a law that all children must go to school."

Trui understands. "Compulsory education – it's about time."

"The school in Harskamp will be overcrowded," Pol retorts.

"Then we'll have to build another classroom," Trui replies calmly.

Pol says no more. He doesn't want another money argument with her. She has strange ideas that the Lord will provide – and, stranger yet, he agrees, for she is right.

CHAPTER TWENTY-THREE

Chapel & Koster

Kamerling takes a trip to attend a wedding, a long distance from Harskamp to deHeide at Noordzeekanaal. He wonders why the place is named after the heather plant, since there is not a sprig of heather to be found at IJmuiden by the North Sea, where a new canal is under construction.

"It was originally called the Heights, but that became deHeide," his hosts explain.

"I wondered if all these shrubs and trees are called heather around here," Kamerling said in jest. "But what an enormous canal they've carved through the dunes here. These people dare to venture a lot!"

"We dare to do even more," Neef, the father of the bride boasts. "We have built this town from the profits of the fishery. And now that the fishing is doing well, we plan on more new houses. Yes, IJmuiden is moving forward!"

"Just in case you have extra money," Kamerling hints, "Harskamp can certainly use some help."

"Ja, ja," Neef nods, "That's the way it is, we went through the same situation here, but now we have an excellent teacher who has helped us start our school and church and Sunday school."

"A church? And who is your dominee?"

Neef laughs. "Actually, since we spent all our own money on the school and the church, with just a bit of help from the government – you know how it is – we just couldn't afford a minister. That's why we hired Jan Brederveld as a lay pastor. He's somewhat conservative, but well liked, and he gets along well with the people of our community."

When Kamerling meets Brederveld and hears him conduct the wedding ceremony, he decides the man would be acceptable in Harskamp – he seems to be serious and learned, as well as amiable and friendly. The schoolmaster ponders ways of persuading him to move there.

Back in Harskamp, plans are made to invite Brederveld to consider the position of chaplain. Kamerling does not like the system by which a congregation makes a call to a minister from another congregation, but he supposes a person is free to decline the call, and sometimes change is a good thing. An invitational letter goes from Harskamp to Mr. Brederveld. He is totally surprised – so surprised, he needs to study the map to find the small dot on the Veluwe called Harskamp.

Jan Brederveld has been a dedicated worker in God's kingdom. From his youth on, he has worked and trained to become a servant of the church. Lacking funds for a seminary education, he obtained permission to work as a lay pastor, an oefenaar, which he enjoys. His wife claims he takes his work too seriously, because he approaches each service with trepidation. However, as soon as he begins to speak, his fears vanish and he draws in his listeners, for he speaks not for himself but for the truth of the Bible. Without lengthy phrases and empty verbiage, his few well-chosen words evoke the greatness of God.

The invitation to Harskamp is irresistible. He feels there is a challenge here that he is eager to meet, more to his liking than a well-established position. He makes the long journey to Harskamp for an interview.

"The man will get along well with the soldiers," Trui remarks later as she discusses her impressions with Mr. Kamerling over a cup of coffee. "Conscientious and devout; he seems to know his Bible."

Kamerling nearly chokes over his coffee. "You haven't been asking him trick questions?"

With a ghost of a smile she says, "You know I wouldn't do that, but I did ask him a few things, and he gave excellent responses. His experience in IJmuiden in setting up the church and school is just what we need here."

Brederveld has lived and worked in IJmuiden for eleven years. The community is now able to hire an ordained dominee, since the fishery has been lucrative. He is attracted to Harskamp, since it is a place where he is needed. He decides to accept the call and will maintain some ties with his former position.

On a quiet evening before Brederveld arrives, Trui wraps her shawl about her shoulders and walks to the new

The Flowering Almond Rod

center. There it is, neatly painted, waiting to welcome its occupants. A double door is central, large double windows on either side and an open porch in front. Above the door the name of the center, "Koningin Wilhelmina," is spelled out in large letters. On the right sits the little chapel, with three narrow windows above the doors and some side windows to provide adequate light. A good-sized house has been provided for chaplain Brederveld and his family: a wife, two sons, and a daughter.

For a long while Trui stands there and thinks about her dreams come true. She can hardly believe it: a home for the soldiers, a chapel, and a chaplain's house. No more church at her house, no more school at her house, no more searching for a preacher every Sunday, responsibility for her sick calls shared – altogether it fills her heart with thanks.

It is hard to believe. Not long ago she stood before a judge, a helpless Veluwe countrywoman, ordered to pay a fine. The people supported her. Martin Luther once stood before a council, and the people stood by him. He said, "Here I stand, I can do no other, God help me." Trui could only tell the judge that she could not do otherwise. She stood alone and God helped her. God helps His children.

Slowly Trui walks home. The shiny bucket hanging on the pump reflects the evening light, and her hand instinctively swings the pump handle. The peace and rest of her home is all she needs.

But unemployment is not to be her lot. Next day, Mr. Kamerling visits. "We have a nice church building, but no koster, and what is a church without a koster? There's the ushering, the foot warmers, a clean glass of water on Sunday...." His eyes twinkle.

"You mean me? In the church?" She sees herself finding places for people, keeping the church – God's house – clean. "I would like to do it. Gladly."

"Ja," says the schoolmaster, "You are still needed, Trui. We want your input whenever we meet; we will hire no one without your vote."

Trui raises her hands in protest. "Sir, stop talking foolishness! That's nonsense!"

Kamerling laughs. He notices her startled expression, but knows for certain that her voice is important in Harskamp. Everyone acknowledges her influence – the only one not confident of this is Trui herself.

On an icy cold day in February, Jan Brederveld is to be installed as chaplain of the Harskamp congregation. Trui has been thinking about an idea for this occasion. Years ago she walked for hours over the heather to hear the inspiring sermons preached by Ds. De Braal; she has used a textbook by de Braal in her school, and now her suggestion that de Braal lead the installation service is agreed upon. What anticipation she feels!

The snow lies deep on the country roads, making travel nearly impossible, but here and there the main roads are cleared. The dominee's carriage cannot reach the church, so he alights and trudges through the deep drifts.

"How beautiful!" he exclaims in admiration of the snow-laden trees.

The farmers, on the other hand, grumble, "What a nuisance! We should have left our horses in the barn and stayed close to the hearth." However, the hearth-loving folks struggle through the snow for the occasion. There has not been much excitement in Harskamp lately.

Trui, the newly appointed koster, bustles about. Her best black apron covers her best black dress; her white ruffled bonnet bobs about as she helps people to their places. "Here's a place for you, please move over, folks. Nelis, there's room if you move into the corner."

"It's so crowded I can hardly draw a breath," complains Nelis.

"Then don't breathe, just make room," Trui retorts.

In the little entry porch she stops some children. "You can't go in until you clean the clumps of snow off your klompen – otherwise you'll ruin the new floor!"

Silence falls over the gathering as Ds. De Braal steps up to the pulpit. His deep voice carries a profound message, still new after more than a thousand years. "By the grace of God did the wise builder lay the foundations."

Trui thumbs through the pages of her Bible. She wants to find the words and commit them to memory. What a great task lies before the new chaplain! By the grace of God he will undertake the work of laying the church's foundation here in Harskamp.

Chaplain Brederveld has forgotten all about the intense cold. His words come forth more easily than he expected, as they always do once he begins. As the words flow, the people listen attentively, for he speaks from his heart. They feel richly blessed after the service is over as they make their way home through the deep snow.

Now that she has taken on the role of koster, Trui waits till everyone is gone. She is convinced that the right man has been selected for the community. Juffrouw Brederveld approaches Trui and inquires about her work. "Is it not too much for you?" she asks quietly. "My daughter Klazien will be glad to help you."

"It's alright for now," replies Trui, "But if it becomes necessary, I appreciate your kind offer."

She glances at young Jacob Brederveld. He wears shoes, not klompen, so there is no need to admonish him not to bring snow into the church. Jacob notices her keen eye and figures she will not tolerate mischief. It was common knowledge that preacher's youngsters were incorrigible rascals.

CHAPTER TWENTY-FOUR

Fulfilment

"No," says the newcomer to Harskamp, a young lady resentful of the fact that her husband's work brought her to this isolated village. "No, vrouw van de Pol, I will not contribute," she replies to Trui's request for money for the school and the church.

Trui is in the habit of carrying a special linen bag in her basket, just in case the opportunity arises for collecting contributions. Sometimes she is surprised.

On her way to a foster home visit, she notices the owner of a renovated house standing in the front yard. Trui's greeting is met with a short nod. The city people do not greet a stranger, much less gossip over the hedge, but for Trui it is only being friendly to stop and talk about the weather and the crops.

"We are newly married and have moved from Amsterdam." She stares into the distance, as if to catch a glimpse of the city. "Far away from here."

"Who are you?" Trui inquires, "I think I saw your husband at the army camp."

The woman nods, controlling her temper. Joop, her husband, told her that the people here were very open in asking questions and not to be offended; their curiosity was meant to be friendly and community-spirited. She replies, "I am Mevrouw van Tienen. My husband is an officer."

"Oh, then you need to live here because of the training exercises," Trui nods. "I can assure you, you won't be sorry, because this is a beautiful place. We love seeing the heather in bloom."

This common countrywoman is speaking to her, Gonda van Tienen, as if she were her equal. This would never happen in the city.

Trui continues, unaware. "Harskamp is a growing community – there was nothing here and now we have a school, a chapel, and a center for the servicemen.

"Ja, ja," Gonda nods, bored, "It's really something."

"Certainly! We've made great strides, but we are still short of money."

Gonda smiles sarcastically. "That seems to be the usual Christian condition."

Trui regards her quizzically. "That's true, I agree, because it means we have to trust in God. When things come too easily, people soon say, 'Thank you, Lord, from now on I won't need you any more.'"

These people living on the Veluwe! So religious! Gonda thinks, then she recalls stories about a certain woman....

"Might you be...?" She hesitates. How in the world do you talk to these country people?

The Flowering Almond Rod

"Ja, you've heard already," Trui helps her, "I am Vrouw van de Pol, formerly Jacoba Geertruida Straatman, previously married to Jan Heebink – but just call me Trui like everyone else does."

"Oh, it was you that had a school here? And you helped with the church and the servicemen's canteen? I have heard amazing stories about you, how everything you did became a success."

"Listen, my dear," Trui sets down her basket, a sign she has something to say. "Don't believe everything you hear." She shakes her head. "People say foolish things. I only help wherever there is a need, and that's all. I just do my duty, no more. Why do people exaggerate these stories? Working in God's fields is its own reward."

Gonda doesn't understand this kind of mindset. Her husband Joop works hard towards a promotion, he is ambitious – that she can understand. She regards Trui with interest – this woman is not ambitious for herself, but at the same time she strives for something beyond personal gain.

"Come and visit sometime," Trui extends a friendly invitation, "The coffee is always ready."

Gonda smiles. "Maybe," she says vaguely, knowing she has no intention of accepting. No, there will be no further contact with the local people, for she will remain Mevrouw van Tienen.

"Will we see you in church on Sunday?" asks Trui.

"I think not; we do not attend church, for we are not Christian believers." She nearly lets on that she and Joop do not want to share a bench with ordinary soldiers. "Sundays are reserved for our time away."

Trui is quiet. She picks up her basket. "I'll be on my way. Pol will be waiting for his coffee. If there is anything you need, just call on me."

Gonda sees her away courteously. This countrywoman is incredible, she thinks. Any need of her? No, she hates churches and pompous preachers, quarrelsome people and boring sermons. What a shame to waste a fine summer day indoors listening to a sermon on Hell and damnation – much more pleasant to be outdoors with Joop, enjoying nature and dreaming about their future. God? Even if he exists, why bother? Leave it to worriers like Trui and peasants who know nothing of the real world. Religion is for simpletons.

When Joop comes home, so handsome in his officer's uniform, Gonda describes her encounter with Trui.

"Thoroughly Veluwse, born and raised here, she knows everything about the village. She seems clever and sharp."

Joop shrugs. "They have some strange beliefs here, so be careful, they may try to convert you to their ways. Keep your distance; before you know it they may trap you into supporting their church and private school and so on."

The young soldiers enjoy the canteen and keep it busy in the evenings, even though some can barely afford sugar for their coffee or tobacco for their clay pipes. Clay pipes were a nineteenth-century fashion, but some carried the habit into the twentieth.

"What do you think?" one asks Brederveld, who is serving coffee while his wife stands by with the sugar pot. "Ja, I'd like very much to have two scoops of sugar in my coffee, but I can't pay for it." The look of suffering on his face turns to laughter as juffrouw Brederveld takes pity on him and adds two scoops to his coffee.

"Now what must I think?" asks Brederveld. In spite of the grey hair hanging limply about his aging face, his piercing look and narrow mouth, Brederveld has the trust of the young men, for they have found him to be fair and honest.

"What's going on, jongens?" asks another soldier.

"You see this cup of coffee I'm holding in my hand? It has just as much sugar as the coffee my mother makes at home – enough to make me forget all my problems."

Juffrouw Brederveld listens to their chatter as she washes cups and prepares more behind the counter. She is happy here – she is fond of the young men and knows how to be firm with them while enjoying their company. She insists they keep the place tidy and homelike. For many it is the first time away from home, and this is how it is meant to be – it is everything they had hoped for.

One fellow noisily drains the last drop of coffee from his cup. "Mmm, delicious!" Brederveld fills his cup again.

Others protest, "Why does he get special favours?"

Brederveld yells above the shouting, "Just come and get it, I'm not a waitress." He directs a comment at some who stay at their table. "Had a long march today? Can't walk any more?"

Shoving his way past the line-up, another grumbles, "I'd rather have something stronger. How about some genever to cheer us up?"

"I thought of that too – coffee makes my mind too dull to ask," comments another.

"A perfect menu would be brown bean hash with bread, then coffee and a drink to follow. We'd sleep well after that." Loud approval sounds through the hall.

Brederveld checks the remaining coffee in the large pot. "This stuff is strong enough to make noisy rebels of you all. You don't even need genever." He remains calm during the grumbling and jeers that follow.

The evening winds up with plans for regular meetings to discuss and debate politics, government, the army, and possibly even religion. No one volunteers to present the first topic, so Brederveld takes it on. "After the debate we'll take a smoke break to clear our minds, and have some singing to finish the evening...." His son comes in. "And Jacob will provide the accompaniment."

"Ja, Jacob," they shout, "Start practicing!"

They drift back to the tables, and the noise continues as they shove chairs around.

"Anyone for a game of chess? Bring out the boards."

"Bread, coffee, beans, and games – what more could we ask?"

"Bible study," scoffs another. He is checked by a rough push on the shoulder.

"Don't ruin a good thing. We like what this place offers."

"Do you want to play the black or white?" The room quiets down as they settle into their games.

Brederveld watches contentedly. This is everything he had hoped — let them talk freely. It shows they feel at home here.

Then he thinks about the growing criticism within the Harskamp community. "Brederveld is our pastor," they say, "And he does his work well — his words are profound, and he also gives hope to his listeners. What we find hard to tolerate is that he spends his weekdays with the soldiers. He stands behind the counter in that canteen as if it is a beer hall. It just isn't fitting for a pastor."

"You people do different things during the week than on Sundays, so why shouldn't he?" Trui asks those gathered under the great tree in the market square. "Our Sundays are special to the Lord, and we do our daily work during the week. It seems to me that the pastor's weekday work goes well at the canteen."

Still, the grumbling continues. A dominee, pastor, oefenaar, or whatever his title, is not an ordinary person and should not stoop to work that is beneath him. This is the way it has always been. An educated man must be respected, and people should be able to look up to him as a tower of righteousness, a rock of strength, a mediator between them and God. It is important to keep to one's place in society or chaos will result.

Such attitudes may also be the reason that the citizens of Harskamp cannot understand Trui. They dislike the fact that she takes leadership, but do not stop her, since they see the good she accomplishes. It has been taken for granted that women are to bear children, cook and scrub, and obey their husbands, perhaps to give up life early after bearing too many children. It has not dawned on the small community that they have a precursor of women's future in Trui's person. Not the shrill, strident voice of the protestors, but the quiet, effective voice of the women who will become leaders in their own fields.

It is not an easy role for Trui. As soon as a problem has been dealt with, another one presents itself. Now the law unexpectedly requires that every child must go to school. The school board meeting goes late; the wives at home suspect there are weighty matters being discussed.

Chairman Knuttel leads the meeting with his usual efficiency. The board organizes a collection and drafts a letter to be circulated among the stakeholders, informing them of the needs of the school. Baron Pallant has offered to sell the school building for twenty-five guilders. Trui brings in coffee and they take a break.

"Trui, sit down a minute," Knuttel suggests.

"No, no," she protests as she hands around the coffee. "There's sugar already in your cups – you dip too deeply into the sugar bowl when you have a chance. I need the sugar for my oatmeal."

"Listen, Trui, you understand how to handle money, and we want your opinion on the school problem." She immediately forgets about the coffee and sits down.

"Is it true that all children must now attend school?" she asks. "There isn't enough room here."

"You are right as usual." Knuttel is amused by her quick perception.

"Ja, man, I read the newspaper."

Harmen Bruil scans his paper. "It says here that the new law goes into effect January 1st next year. Well, coffee drinkers, we will have to prepare. I think we'll have to add another room to the school." "If we buy the building," says Teunis the treasurer, "It will soon be too small, but if we pay for an addition, the cost will be the same."

A lengthy discussion, with Trui included, follows. The new law will bring in additional enrolment, but the space to accommodate more children will be the board's responsibility.

"If we buy the building," Knuttel suggests, "We can use volunteers to construct the addition. We should find an architect to design an inexpensive plan, and then do our own carpentry and painting."

They trust that the money will appear, from where they do not yet know, but it is unthinkable that the children would have to go elsewhere for lack of space. The local government cannot be asked for aid, but Knuttel knows of a bank in Ede where they can get a mortgage. The arrangements are agreed upon and fundraising begins anew. They are less desperate this time, since the church is well attended and people have more to give. A mortgage is something new for Trui – she does not like the idea but understands that it is a necessary evil.

At the same meeting, Kamerling urgently requests an assistant teacher. Previous advertisements have resulted in applicants who left after a month, or who enjoyed their genever too well and had to be dismissed.

"I can hardly blame them when they leave for better-paying positions," Knuttel remarks.

Meeuwis Bouw, who seldom speaks but is a keen observer, says in his slow, deep voice, "Young people don't understand their gifts are from God, to be shared generously – they work only for their financial gain."

"Not all young teachers are like that," Knuttel defends them. "If an assistant has the opportunity for advancement, he should move onward."

Yes, they would agree it would be an acceptable condition of employment. Kamerling is permitted to seek further for assistance. He thinks of his six years of continual searching. It is not good to have so many changes.

The next item on the agenda concerns the new handicraft teacher Juffrouw Bos, Trui's new assistant. Trui feels she is getting too old to keep up with the latest trends. "Women used to knit their own socks and sweaters, but now they want to learn to crochet and cross-stitch, which

The Flowering Almond Rod

I can't teach. There are too many new pupils to manage alone." Juffrouw Bos is not certified but does take lessons. Trui observes her doubtfully. The girl tries hard, but she has never knitted a pair of socks, so how could she even mend them? Times are changing – certificates aren't necessary for knitting and mending.

The time has come for building. The board meets often. The great moment arrives when the chairman signs his name in large letters on the document at the notary's office in Ede – the building is now owned by the society for Christian education in Harskamp. As he strokes the pen over the paper, he counts the years of hard work and saving that have gone into this moment.

The children are happy. The people of the town often stroll by to watch the construction and to see if the building looks more like a school. Now it has three classrooms, and, facing the road, an impressive double door crowned by a beautiful gabled façade. Trui is pleased best of all with the stone engraving above the door that reads, "SCHOOL MET DEN BIJBEL." Above that is carved the year "Anno 1901."

Trui lingers over her evening meditation, thinking of the years gone by. How often has she sat here with her little booklet? She is seventy-three and beginning to feel her age. For countless years her evenings have been spent thinking of the joys and sorrows, the problems and solutions of the day. The rebuilding of the school, the School with the Bible, is completed, and it seems too wonderful to comprehend, almost beyond belief.

Is anything too much for God? Can a believer ask anything of Him? She gazes without seeing what is before her, but rather she sees the life behind her. Her efforts have been rewarded, richer and greater in fulfillment than anything she had ever imagined.

She had suffered scorn and laughter, but she always knew she worked for the kingdom of God. Through toil in the heat of the midday, through struggles over barren ground, she held to the unshakeable faith that she must do what was necessary for God's children. This evening marks the close of the most important part of her life; her mission has ended.

She maintains ties with the school and admits the help of juffrouw Bos is quite welcome. The days feel long, for there is much to keep her busy. She continues to visit the sick and supervise the foster children's care. There are grandchildren and great-grandchildren to enjoy.

Pol has aged greatly. He sleeps most of the day in his chair and is more care than company. He is past his eightieth year, and his candle burns low. This is how life ends, thinks Trui. Soon my work will be done, and then how much time is left? She is shaken when she wonders if her life's task is really over. What then?

Juffrouw Bos still lacks accreditation, so Trui continues to teach handcrafts. The school board, the schoolmaster, and the chaplain still meet in her dark house. The

The Flowering Almond Rod

old wicker chairs creak and the coffee perks contentedly as matters concerning the school, the canteen, and the chapel are sorted and settled.

Chaplain Brederveld — his is a good family. His wife has the respect of the community, his daughter Klazien is a friendly girl, and mischievous Jacob will someday become a good teacher.

The Lord will use me as long as I am on this earth; the work is never finished, there is always something to be done. She thinks about Brederveld's sister, who has moved in with the family — a woman who will not take religion seriously in spite of many entreaties. Trui engages her in conversation under the trees in front of the canteen. "Ja," says the woman, "My brother likes it here — a good house, a pleasant chapel, beautiful surroundings. It suits him well."

Trui agrees. "The heather is lovely, but we don't have a house and a church for pleasure only, to take or leave as we choose. Those who struggled in the past to build this place understand better."

The sister looks perplexed. "You are very serious about this." She laughs. "You don't belong to one of those narrow-minded downhearted groups, do you?"

Trui's eyebrows lift. "Do I look downhearted? I am just a child of God, nothing more or less. I read in the Bible there is no need to be sad, because we can draw freely from the well of living water every day. How can that be downhearted?" Trui regards her thoughtfully. "Do you not believe in anything?"

The sister shrugs. "Ach, come on, I live a good life and that's enough."

"You don't believe the Bible? Surely you were brought up to believe."

"Oh, ja," she replies hastily, "I had a good Christian upbringing, and hear about it every day in my brother's house. I just can't be bothered with all that folderol."

Trui thinks about the hard-earned place where they stand.

Obviously the Lord helped; he helped in dire need, the visible signs stood right before them. How could one see this and not believe? It was beyond understanding.

"If you don't believe in the Bible, we can talk for days without understanding each other. Let us just leave it there. I only hope that someday you will reach for God's help and guidance through the Bible. I bid you goodbye now, but you are welcome to visit me any time you like."

Trui journeys homeward, her energetic walk somewhat slower, but her spirit still strong. Is her work finished? The answer is clear: there is much still to be done.

On the 2nd day of February, 1902, Jan van de Pol departs this life, two days before turning eighty-five. Two elderly people living peacefully, expecting their children for a day of celebration, who have shared happiness and sorrow – suddenly the end arrives and Trui's husband is taken away. Bewildered, she sees his rosy complexion turn gray, his pipe drop from his hand, and his mouth stiffen. "Jan..." she stammers, "Is this also over?" She leans over his cold face. He was neither a cheerful companion nor a hard worker, but yet... she will miss him. This is the end, Lord, she prays, my work is done.

CHAPTER TWENTY-FIVE

Fifty Guilders

Now another issue requites attention – the schoolmaster Kamerling has responded to an advertisement for a headmaster in Rinsumageest. "I can't see myself staying in the same place my whole life," he confides to Trui. "Rinsumageest calls me – there is much work to be done there, while on the other hand, all runs smoothly here."

Trui understands; he has youth and energy to offer. Rinsumageest has need of someone who will put forth the effort to meet the needs of the school and community. Kamerling's resignation as of August is met with dismay and great disappointment in Harskamp. His service to the school and to the church services in Trui's house will always be remembered. But now the school and church and military canteen are in place, and no one can blame him for seeking a new challenge.

"I will write you a letter every now and then about the way it goes here," Trui promises. Kamerling accepts her promise with a smile, for Trui is famous for her letters to her married children and anyone else to whom she has anything to say. Her lengthy, detailed letters tell of the care and concern she has poured into lives of all around her.

A new headmaster; a new concern. Inquiries reveal a promising candidate by the name of Wormgoor, who heads a school in Zutphen, so Teunis Onderstel (now chairman), Harmen Bruil, and Meeuwis Bouw undertake a journey. If this individual suits the needs of the Harskamp school, overtures can be made.

Meester Wormgoor is surprised.

"Don't get us wrong," says Onderstel, "But just in case you'd like a change, we will be needing a new hoofdmeester in Harskamp."

They are invited to inspect the building and management of the school in Zutphen and are suitably impressed — it seems to be well run. The children are courteous and show no fear of their elders.

They meet in the office. Meeuwis Bouw explains, "Our first priority is to educate according to God's word. We have struggled for years to achieve Christian education and feel it must be maintained." He regards Wormgoor from under his heavy eyebrows. "We must agree on that before we proceed any further."

"I am deeply amazed," replies Wormgoor. "I am ready to make a change, but the one thing that holds me back is the fact that I now have a place in a good Christian school."

Teunis Onderstal laughs in surprise. "Just wait and see. You will be so very welcome in Harskamp."

Ge Verhoog

Everything comes together like slates on a roof; the meeting moves to the meester's home, where they are given a warm welcome by mevrouw Wormgoor.

There is a mood of joyful accord as they journey home. "The Lord has guided our way," says Meeuwis Bouw. "We can only work and pray and wait for the Lord's blessing."

Wormgoor and his wife travel to Harskamp, an important step in their decision. Will the salary and living conditions compare favourably? Zutphen is a fair-sized city, while Harskamp is small and isolated. Meester Wormgoor is businesslike, but also idealistic; he sees the situation clearly and decides that he is willing and able to meet the needs of this community.

So, in August of 1902, meester Kamerling moves on and is replaced by meester Wormgoor. He will lead the school for thirty-two successful years.

In Ede, de heer Horstman reads his newspaper; he is still intrigued by the news from Harskamp. Those people continue on, he notes ironically. Where do they get the stubborn notion that they must do everything themselves and pay the entire cost, when they could have a free public school? It has to be the influence of those eccentric intellectuals, those impoverished professional educators who live for their ideals, existing on meagre wages, bearing contempt and scorn.

Horstman just cannot understand what motivates them. The teachers actually bear the greatest burden of the Christian School Movement – their salaries are barely adequate, they work with sub-standard buildings and materials, and adversaries ridicule them.

He gazes out of the high windows at his immaculate flower garden. No, he cannot understand those teachers – such zealots. For an instant he cannot understand himself either, for somewhere, deep down, he feels respect for the courage they reveal when they live by their principles....

The year 1902 brings another change: Trui is aging. Her fiery energy has dwindled, and the noisy handcraft classes tire her. She has always loved working with the children, but often finds them too active to manage.

"Please understand," Teunis Onderstel speaks for the school board, "I know we are men of few words—"

"Then don't say anything," Trui replies with a smile. "I know your message, and I believe this is the way things should be. I have been teaching for thirty-three years." She stares out of the little window. "What a long time, and yet it went so quickly. It was work that had to be done, so I did what I could."

A quiet time of reminiscence falls upon those two veterans as they sit in the little house on the sandy road. They have struggled toward the same goal, dealt with officials, overcome endless setbacks, kept to their thankless tasks, and now they see how Harskamp has grown and prospered.

"I always knew that the Lord must come first," says Trui pensively. "He must increase and I must decrease." She smiles briefly. "It is true, my life is dwindling away." She thinks of the many days she has lain in bed with a persistent cold. More and more she finds it difficult to get up in the morning, and earlier then ever retires with her devotional book – her years are telling.

What did Jannetje say recently? "You should leave Harskamp and come and live with our family so you won't be all alone. We would like very much to have you live here."

Trui is not yet ready to accept the invitation. "I manage all right on my own." She knows the time will come, but to leave Harskamp? It seems her work is nearing its end – this evening's message would make it official.

"We have found an excellent assistant administrator who is ambitious and plans to stay here. Juffrouw Wormgoor can handle your handcraft classes if they are too much for you."

Trui nods slowly. And so, her work in the school is finally done. It has to be this way, but still it hurts. It is not easy to retire.

She receives a formal letter from the board expressing much appreciation for her years of work, with a note attached to inform her that her salary of fifty guilders per year has been terminated. How strange it feels.

Then she smiles. Oh, she received the fifty guilders, but where did it go? Right back to the school, the church, and the servicemen's canteen.

CHAPTER TWENTY-SIX

Trui's Work Is Done

Evening falls quickly over Trui's life. There are many things she cannot do anymore. When her children come to visit, they often find her in bed. "Nothing in particular," she replies to their concerns. "I just did too much yesterday. I am tired." The children worry about her living alone. Again Jannetje suggests carefully that she should come and live at her home.

"Dear Mother, you have worked for others all your life and you've been so busy. It's time to rest and let us take care of you. We would love to have you in our home."

"And me, sitting in a soft chair with idle hands in my lap?" Trui resists. "Just looking out of the window, doing nothing? How could you think it?"

"No, moeder," Jannetje tries to convince her. "You could knit for my boys, socks and sweaters. I never get around to doing it."

"Never get around to it? I knitted for all you children when you were small and did a lot of other things besides."

"I mean—"

Trui nods agreeably. "Listen, girl, be straightforward. I know what you mean, but the Lord is telling me to rest because my work in Harskamp is finished. Why else would I be tired and ill so often?" By speaking these words aloud, she is finally able to say goodbye to her house, her yard, her sandy path, and her school in the annex of the barn. What a paradise of memories!

Paradise. While her life was often far from it, she now sees it in the light of the ever-present help of God. Her earthly paradise. Parting will be hard, but she must be firm. This part of her life is finished, she must look forward, and as long as the Lord gives her life, she must serve Him.

Her final appearance in the school is to attend the annual meeting. For the first time they are out of debt, and there is even a little money to spare. For Trui's farewell gathering, they can even enjoy a treat of currant buns with the coffee.

"I thought my currant bun should taste bitter, since it is the last one I'll have here in Harskamp," Trui makes light of the occasion, "But it is delicious anyway."

Meester Wormgoor regards her thoughtfully. What a great person in God's kingdom, he thinks. So modest, a true child of God.

No more debt, even a little money to spare – how rich we are, Trui thinks. Now I am sure, I feel it, that things will go well. God has blessed the work of our hands. At home in her house for the last evening, she reads from psalm 90.

"Lord, you have been our dwelling place from one generation to the next. We end our years as a dream, our days seventy or eighty years and the greater part is spent in toil and sorrow. Let us count our days and become wise. Let your work be known to your servants and your glory to your children and bless the work of our hands."

Trui moved to Ede in 1903 to live with her daughter. She died on Tuesday, June 20, at the age of seventy-eight years.

Scanned from original documents in
possession of Trui Straatman's descendants.

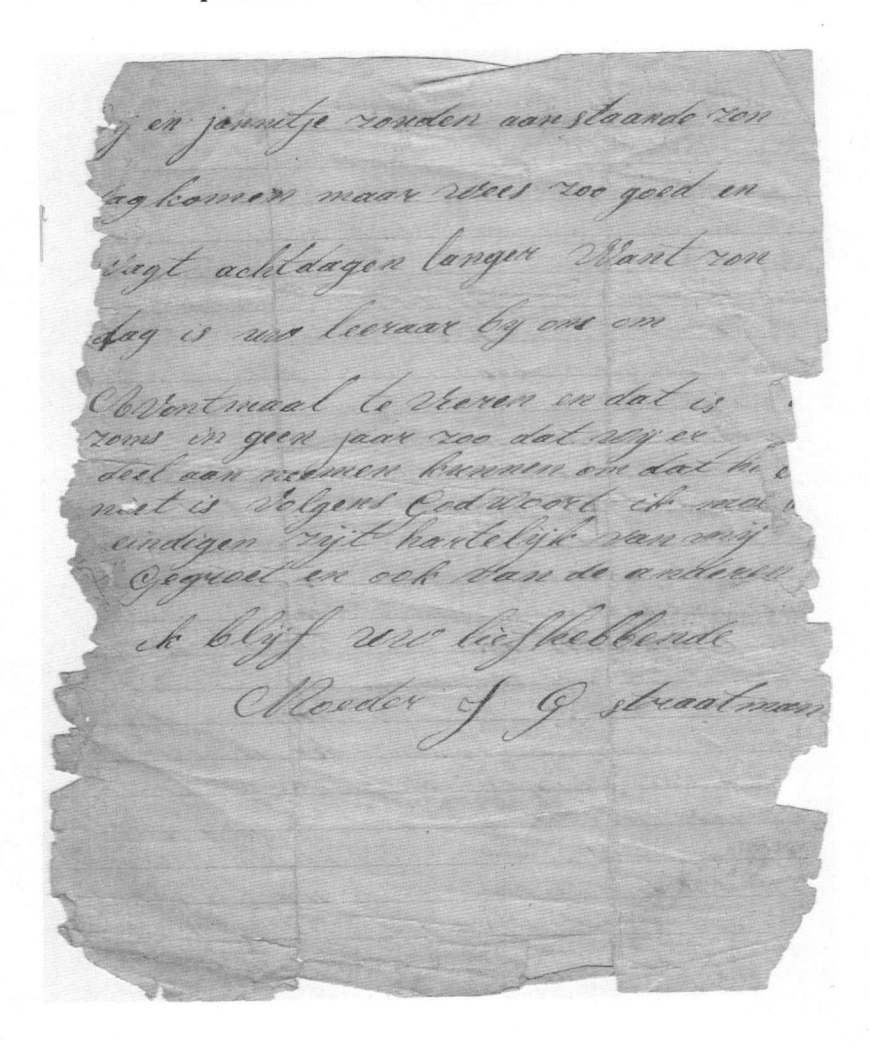

[handwritten letter fragment, partially legible:]

> en jannitje zouden aanstaande zon-
> dag komen maar wees zoo goed en
> zegt achtdagen langer Want zon-
> dag is uw leeraar by ons om
> Avontmaal te vieren en dat is
> zoms in geen jaar zoo dat wij er
> deel aan nemen kunnen om dat het
> niet is volgens Gods woord ik wil
> eindigen zijt hartelijk van mij
> gegroet en ook van de andere
>
> ik blijf uw liefhebbende
> Moeder J G straatman

A fragment of a letter by Trui to one of her children showing her beautiful handwriting.

TRANSLATOR'S NOTE

De Bloeiende Amandeltak, written in Dutch by Ge Verhoog, first appeared in 1975 in The Calvinist Contact, a Canadian newspaper published by and for post-war immigrants from the Netherlands. It is the story of an impoverished widow, Trui Straatman, who set up a school in her home when none was available to the children of the little community of Harskamp on the Veluwe in the Netherlands. She was determined that people should be able to read the bible for themselves and convinced that literacy was a necessary tool for this purpose. Trui's determination is rooted in her deep faith and influenced by the Christian philosophy of her time.

In North America today the Christian school movement is strong and growing. I believe that the grass roots movement to establish independent Christian schools in the Netherlands is where it all started. Trui Straatman's little home school grew into a flourishing establishment still operating today in the town of Harskamp. A recent biography of Abraham Kuyper, Christian philosopher, clergyman and politician, one-time prime minister of the Netherlands shows how influential his thinking was in the establishment of Christian schools.

Ge Verhoog

The story is a work of fiction based on historical information. Included among the real life characters were my grandfather Meeuwis Bouw, his brother Jan and their mother Elberthe. My mother, Hendrika Bouw Schuld, excited to see this story in print, began the work of translating it into English in 1975. It was forgotten until just recently when I found her manuscript among my late brother's books. I felt it was a story worth sharing and therefore spent the past year completing and rewriting the translation.

Heartfelt thanks go to Tony Maan, pastor of Maranatha Christian Reformed Church in Lethbridge, Alberta, for his scholarly introduction to the history of the Netherlands during the time of this story, and for his encouragement and help throughout the project. Many thanks also to Berthe, Gert, Marie and Mr. Amerongen for showing me all the places in which the story took place and for sharing the original documents preserved by Trui Straatman's family.

Evelyn Sterenberg

The Flowering Almond Rod

A Christian school group ca. 1912 in Gelderland near Bennekom. Hendrika Bouw is in the middle row, third from the right. She is wearing a black bow because her mother recently died. After he moved away from Harskamp, Meeuwis Bouw was instrumental in founding this school, serving as board chairman.

Printed in Canada